A STAIRWAY TO

DANGER

A Shakertown Adventure - Book 1

by Ben Woodard

To Breccan

Ben Woodard

A Stairway To Danger

Ben Woodard

© 2013

All Rights Reserved

Historical Fiction

Cover Design: Trifecta

Summary: An eyeless body and a rusty barge immerse two small town boys in a harrowing mystery.

ISBN: 978-0-9886274-1-3

Published by: Miller-Martin Press, Lexington, KY

In memory of my dad who grew up in Shakertown and whose adventures inspired this book.

Other Books By Ben Woodard

The Boy Who Flew With Eagles - a middle grade short novel

Steps Into Darkness, A Shakertown Adventure Book 2 - a young adult novel

A Terrible Price - a middle grade short story

The Hunt - a young adult short story

The Trestle - a young adult short story

The African saying claims it takes a village to raise a child. That may be true, but I'm sure it takes a ton of friends to write a book. At least in my case.

Thank you, Marcia for your wisdom and experience. You made the book more than I ever thought it could be.

Much appreciation goes to my readers Harry, Ron, and JD, for your insights and tough criticism.

Thanks Kevin for hard work and imaginative thinking on the cover and illustrations.

High fives to my critique group, Martha, Karen, Harry, Evelyn, Debbie, Heather, Elane, Sharon, and Dan. You guys are great.

Thanks so much Barbara. Your edit taught me more than I've learned from writing classes.

A special thanks to Karen L., my "clean up hitter." Your last look at the book gave it the polish it needed.

Most of all, love and thanks to my wife, Lynda. You read and re-read the story until your eyes turned red. This book would never have been finished without your help.

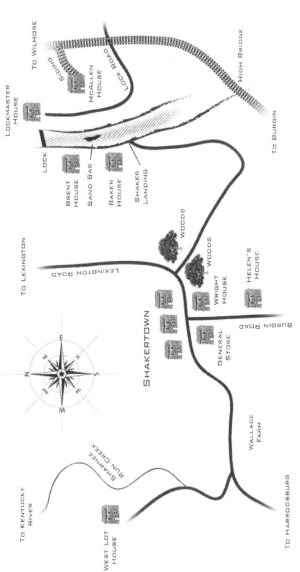

A STAIRWAY TO

DANGER

CHAPTER
One

Will rolled the body over with his boot. An arm flopped in the water and the face pointed directly at Tom. A face with no eyes. Tom sucked in his breath and staggered back. He slumped to his knees staring at the ground.

"Fish ate em," Will said, toeing the body.

Tom's stomach rolled like the back of a hay wagon, and the taste of bile filled his mouth. His breath came in short gasps as his mind raced back to that narrow staircase four years ago. He felt those walls closing in again. Sweat rolled down the nape of his neck. He bent over, gagged, and threw up. He wanted to empty out all his guilt and self-loathing onto the rocky hillside.

"His face is all eat up, but he looks like the Deputy." Will said. "He's been missing a couple of days. We better tell the Sheriff."

Tom couldn't answer. He wanted to run. Run and not stop. Run north until he collapsed somewhere on the way to Cincinnati. He had to get away. Now.

Will slipped his arms under Tom's armpits and hefted him up like a sack of potatoes. "Let's get outta here. I'm getting kinda sick myself."

The yellow sky darkened to purple as they edged past the body and moved along the bank, following the river back toward Shakertown. Tom looked away from the bloated corpse and tried not to breathe. The stench filled the night air suffocating the musty smells of the river and forest. Tom didn't recognize the Deputy, but he recognized death. He had hoped coming to the farm would help him forget what happened at Grandfather's, but reminders were everywhere.

As they picked their way through the mud and rocks along the bank, Tom's thoughts swirled in his head. Since leaving the farm in the early afternoon, they'd searched for gold. Shaker gold. Not a dead body.

Ever since Will first mentioned the story of the Shakers hiding their gold during the Civil War, Tom had pestered him to hunt for it. They had slogged down the creek after finishing their farm chores hoping to be home before dark. But caves and crevasses took time to search and now it would be after ten before they reached Shakertown.

Then they'd have to find somebody in the village with a phone to call the Sheriff. Mr. Glancy at the corner store had one, and Tom's uncle, but Uncle Davis's house was further away. Few people in the small village needed, or wanted, a telephone.

Tom shook his head trying to forget the image of the dead Deputy. Seeing the body brought back a memory he'd tried to forget.

Will interrupted his thoughts. "What's on your mind, little cuz?"

"The Deputy. Seeing the body sure got to me. Could you tell what killed him?"

"Naw, I didn't look that close. I only seen one other body. Feller fell off a barn roof. Nobody found him for a couple of days. He wasn't eat up like this one, but he stunk bad. I had to help carry him to the wagon."

"I'd rather forget about bodies. Let's talk about the gold," Tom said.

"Don't get your hopes up. The story of Shaker gold has been around for years and lots of folks have searched for it. They say that the Shakers hid it during the Civil War so none of the armies could get it. Strange people, not marrying or nothing, but good businessmen and they made a bunch of money. Daddy said he and your daddy looked everywhere when they were boys. Nobody found nothing."

Tom sighed.

"That don't mean it ain't here. You got ideas. Mostly crazy ones, but sometimes you're right. If anybody could find the gold, you could."

"I'd like to," said Tom. "And use the money to get out of town. Not much chance of that happening though."

They both got quiet concentrating on their footing in the dark. Debris from the river and rocks from the palisade cliffs littered the ground. Tom grunted as he climbed through fallen tree limbs and logs wiping the cobwebs off his face. Finally, the sound of water pouring over the lock dam reached them. Shaker Landing and the road to Shakertown were near.

As they passed the lock, Tom noticed a large, dark shadow on the other side of the river. "Is that the barge?"

"Yeah. Ain't seen it before. Heard people talking about it. Nobody seems to know if it was brought here or if it's a derelict."

"And nobody tried to find out?"

"Everybody ain't as nosy as you."

"Curious. Not nosy."

"Whatever you want to call it."

Tom stiffened. "Look," he said. "A light, on the barge."

"I don't see nothing."

An icy chill wormed its way down Tom's spine. "I swear there was a light, Will," he said. "And there's something weird about that barge."

"What?"

"I ...," Tom hesitated.

Will grabbed his arm. "Spit it out. What did you see?"

"Only a light, but the barge is supposed to be deserted. Why is someone there with a light? Do you think that barge could have something to do with the Deputy's death?"

"Huh? Another one of your hunches?"

"Maybe."

"Most of the time you're wrong."

Tom rubbed his chin. "Probably this time too, but I'd like to find out why that rusty old thing is here."

"Not much chance of that. We got too much farm work to do."

As Tom brushed aside branches and slogged again toward the Landing, Will yanked him back, finger to his lips.

"What?" Tom whispered as Will pulled him behind a boulder. Seconds later bushes near them rustled. The two crouched low as a silhouette emerged out of the murk in front of them. A huge man lumbered towards them. Tom's stomach lurched as the dark figure passed within inches of their hiding place. They waited, frozen, until they could no longer hear a noise above the sound of the water. Slowly, Will straightened and glanced around.

"Who do you think that was?" Tom asked panting.

Will let out a soft whistle. "Never seen anybody that big around here. Scary looking."

Tom exhaled softly. "You think that giant had something to do with the Deputy's death?"

"I don't know. What's with you? First the barge, and now this guy. Forget it. It was just an accident."

"Maybe," said Tom, "but there's lots of strangers around. Something's happening."

"A new business, Daddy said. He didn't know what."

"Why start a business in this backwater?" asked Tom.

"Why not? Shakertown's not a bad place. You only been here three months. Give it a chance. And, think about it, we have the river and the railroad. The Shakers thought it was a great place for their business."

"See what it got them. They're all gone, and now your family owns a hunk of their old land."

"What do you mean, *your* family? It's yours, too."

Tom was quiet. "Yeah,"

But only Will seemed like family. Will's father, Uncle Davis, hardly spoke to him, and he never saw Aunt May. Since his arrival at the farm, he'd spent every day going to school and working on the farm. Every night he and Will slept in the attic of the West Lot house. Unless he could get a little money, that was going to be his life. Will liked it. He didn't.

"C'mon," said Will as he scrambled up on the road. "Let's get outta here before that guy comes back."

As he followed his cousin, Tom glanced back at the dark shadow of the barge. A light blinked. The chill in his bones returned.

Something was going on down there. Something bad.

CHAPTER
TWO

The next morning Tom yawned as he shuffled behind Will through the knee-high pasture grass. After reaching town last night, they'd pounded on the door of the General Store waking Mr. Glancy who lived in the back. The storekeeper called the Sheriff who rounded up some men to get the body.

The lawman kept the boys at the store past midnight asking them questions. Tom was surprised by the Sheriff's appearance. He had seen the officer in Nicholasville a year or so before. The man looked different now—worse. Crows feet framed his eyes and his lips set in a tight grimace. And he picked at his fingernails while talking. He had ignored their mention of the mysterious stranger.

As they neared the village, Tom jerked wide awake. Laughter and yelling grabbed his attention. A husky boy in mud-covered overalls shoved an old Negro man while two other boys stood by snickering.

"Junior Baker is acting up again," said Will.

"Why are they picking on that old man?"

"Because they can. Junior is a bully and a coward. Just like his dad, Leon."

"Come on, let's stop them. We can handle those guys."

"Nah, don't get involved. Can't go helping out a Negro against a white man no matter what he's doing. People wouldn't like it."

As they watched, a redheaded whirlwind in a blue dress charged out of a nearby house and rushed up to the tall boy and jabbed her finger in the big kid's chest.

Tom stood open-mouthed. He'd never seen Helen quite like this.

Will chuckled. "Junior's met his match now."

The three boys backed away from the girl's onslaught, and the elderly man limped down the street. Helen's hands flew to her hips and she glared at the retreating boys.

"Who's the old man?" asked Tom. "I saw him the first time I went into town."

"Jefferson."

"Is that his first or last name?"

"I don't know. Everybody just calls him Jefferson."

"I'm glad Helen stopped them."

Tom gawked at the girl, then noticed Will's smirk. Tom's ears reddened.

"Why don't you ask her out?" asked Will.

"Who?"

"Don't give me that," said Will. "I know you're sweet on her. You look at her like a wide-eyed puppy staring at a steak bone."

"Haven't got time. Your dad will be working me to death the next three months with school out. And I've got to do a good job."

"Don't worry, he ain't gonna kick you out. He loves having another unpaid hand. He'll let us off work on Sunday. Go visit her then."

Tom shook his head.

"Well, it ain't likely she'd go out with you anyway, since she's always turning me down."

Tom snorted.

Helen spotted them, turned and waved. They waved back, and she started toward them. Tom's heart went to his throat.

Helen's red face mirrored her hair and both her fists were clenched.

"That Junior Baker," she said. "One of these days ..."

"Gonna hurt him, are you?" Will grinned at her.

Her face got redder. "I didn't see you doing anything."

Will glanced down. "Daddy wouldn't like it if I beat up Leon's boy."

Helen rolled her eyes.

"You know Tom, don't you?" said Will. "He's from Nicholasville and is living with me in the West Lot house and working on the farm. He's a Wallace too."

She smiled and nodded at Tom.

"Hey," she said. "I just heard about Deputy Roland. You found him?"

"Yeah," said Will. "We were hiking down Shawnee Run. He'd washed ashore there."

"You were there too?" she said looking at Tom, her eyes wide.

He nodded.

"We woke up Mr. Glancy and waited for the Sheriff," said Will. "We were still there when they brought the body in, wrapped up in an old tarp. All the men had bandanas covering their noses."

Helen ran her fingers through her hair. "How awful."

"Yeah," said Will.

The three stood lost in their thoughts as a flock of crows in a nearby tree squawked their complaints.

"So what are you two doing?"

"Headin' back to the house," said Will. "Got the rest of the day off."

Tom nodded.

Helen pointed to Tom, and said, "Does he speak?"

Tom's face burned.

Will laughed. "He don't get out much. But as far as I know he *can* talk."

Tom scowled at Will. "Hi Helen," he said.

She laughed. A friendly laugh.

"I think he's just awed by your beauty," said Will.

"You're full of it, Will. I'm going to need hip boots to get out of here. See you later."

As she headed home, Will said, "Hey Helen, you want to go down to Shaker Landing and look at the old barge with us?"

She raised her eyebrows. "Us? Me with both of you? And why do you want to look at the barge?"

"We're curious why it's there. It was Tom's idea."

She gave Tom a smile he swore lit up the village. "I have to ask my mother first."

"Your mother knows me," said Will.

"That's why I have to ask her," she said with a wink to Tom.

The three ambled to Helen's house where her mother

pushed open the screen door and frowned at Helen's request. "Dear, a lady doesn't go off with *two* gentlemen."

"Aw, Mama, you know Will, and Tom is his cousin. And besides they're not gentlemen."

"That's what I'm afraid of," said her mother sternly, but with a half smile.

"I knew your family, Tom. Your mother and father were fine people. I'm sorry for all the tragedy you've had."

Tom swallowed, and he mumbled, "Thanks."

Helen's mother nodded and went back into the house.

"I need to change my clothes," said Helen. "Just come back in a bit."

As the boys shuffled home to the West Lot house, Tom asked, "What was that all about?"

"It just popped into my head. You wanted to see the old barge in daylight and now you get a chance to spend time with Helen. I knew you weren't going to ask her yourself."

"You lie darn good. You didn't do it for me, did you? You wanted to be with her."

Will grinned. "I'll take care of you, little cuz, but I don't understand you. You act like you'll try anything, but you're afraid to talk to a girl?"

"Girls make me nervous."

"Haven't been around many of them, have you? Helen

is one healthy heifer. We raise em good here in Shakertown, but be a little more subtle. I thought your eyes were going to burn a hole in her dress."

Tom shuffled his feet, eyeing the ground.

"What's the matter? Afraid she won't look at you with me around?"

"No." Tom's shoulders drooped. "Why did she say that?"

"What?"

"Mrs. Hardy, about my family."

"She didn't mean anything. Just trying to be nice. That's what people do. Don't be so cranky."

Tom glared at Will and stalked across the yard, yanking open the door to the house. The smell of sweat and cooking greeted him. This was his home now—the three story Shaker-built house owned by the Wallace family.

The boys trudged upstairs to their room under the eaves and pulled on clean clothes. Tom dug out a brass spyglass his father had brought back from Cuba during the Spanish-American War. On the way out they passed Aunt Bessie's room and told her they'd be back in time for dinner.

They picked up Helen and the three wandered down the gravel road toward Shaker Landing. Dark cumulus clouds rolled into the river valley from the West causing shadows to creep across the placid river. As they reached the river, Tom noticed a dead carp washed up on the bank, bleached white by the sun. His pulse raced thinking of the Deputy's body. Even living in the graveyard house with his grandfather, he had never seen a dead body up close—until that one Sunday morning four years ago. His stomach churned and he looked away from the fish.

The barge was anchored a half mile downstream from the landing, but on the opposite side. A lockmaster's house, now abandoned, sat beside the closed lock. The road to the house traveled past the barge, but the passageway was blocked by landslides from the cliff above.

Several houses stood abandoned along the dirt road. Others, having escaped high water damage, were still occupied. At least until the next flood. The Baker family lived in one, and Tom was glad to see Junior wasn't around.

When the rough road ended, the three picked their way along the bank through the trees and briars until they got opposite the barge. A large flat rock overlooking the river provided a perch to observe the barge. Turkey vultures circled in the cloud-splattered sky, and crappie drew circles in the water.

"Wow," said Helen. "It looks awful. All covered with rust."

"Yeah," said Will, "and the wheel house is about to fall

off. What do you see, little cuz?"

Tom slid the spyglass open and fiddled with the lens. Just as the image sharpened into focus, a voice boomed behind them.

"What are you kids doing here?"

They spun around to see an immense man in dirty overalls and a floppy hat. A single gold tooth gleamed in the sunshine. He leveled a rifle at them.

CHAPTER
Three

"You're on private property," the hulking man said. "Get."

The three slid off the rock and warily moved past the man.

"The pretty girl can stay." He leered at Helen. The glint of the gold tooth drew Tom to the leathery face. Hard eyes burned above the lecherous mouth.

Helen's eyes flashed. "I'd rather—" she started.

"She'd rather go home to her parents," interrupted Will as he grabbed her arm pulling her away. "They're expecting her."

"Ow," said Helen. "You're hurting me, Will."

"Hush." Will hissed.

Will released Helen when they were out of sight of the huge man. Tom's face was red and he glared at Will.

"Calm down," said Will, "I ain't gonna hurt your sweetie."

Helen's face matched Tom's. "I don't like being yanked around, Will."

"Sorry, I didn't mean to be so rough, but don't ever argue with a man carrying a gun. That lug was serious. He had the eye of a killer."

"The same guy we saw at the river. A guard," said Tom.

"Yeah, it was him," said Will. "And you're right. Some kind of guard."

"Toothy," said Tom.

Will chuckled. "Good name for him."

"A guard, for what?" said Helen.

"Don't know," said Will.

"We saw him not far from where we found Deputy Roland," said Tom.

Helen's hand went to her mouth. "We have to tell the Sheriff."

"It's too late," said Will, eyeing the sun dropping behind the Palisades. "We don't have time to go all the way to Harrodsburg."

"Won't have to," said Helen, "he's in the village today. Daddy told me he was meeting with some folks down at Glancy's. We might catch him before he goes home."

"We better hustle, then," said Will.

The three friends picked up the pace and a half hour

later found Sheriff Jamison talking to several men outside the general store.

"Sheriff," said Will, "got a minute?"

"That's about all I got," the man said, his lips tight. "What do you need?"

"Any news about Deputy Roland?" asked Will.

The burly man nodded. "Fractured skull. Looks like he fell and hit his head. We found his fishing gear nearby."

They told him about the incident down at the river. His face flushed in anger.

"I don't know who that was, but you need to stay away. All the land along the river is in private hands now. They don't want nobody around. That's their right. You shouldn't have been there last night either."

"He looked like he was guarding something," said Tom. "But there didn't seem to be anything worth guarding."

"That's none of your business," the Sheriff said spitting out the words.

Puzzled at the Sheriff's angry answer, Tom asked in a quiet voice, "Who bought the land?"

The Sheriff's face got redder. He bent down, his eyes boring into Tom's.

"Boy, you know what they say about curiosity and the cat? You better be careful. Who owns that land is something else that just ain't your business."

Tom seethed. He knew public records listed land ownership. He stepped back and said, "Sir, we can go to the courthouse and find out."

"I wouldn't advise it."

The three exchanged glances. Sheriff Jamison unclenched his fists.

"There's no reason to go snooping around the courthouse. New folks moved into the old McAllen house across the river. They bought all the land down there on both sides. Everything. Even most of those old houses in the bottom that get flooded. And since the lock is closed, they bought the lockmaster's house.

I went up to talk to them and they seem like fine folks, but private. They don't want to be bothered by nobody. I don't understand, but that's their right. So whatever you're thinking, forget it. And leave them alone. You do something stupid, and I'll put you in jail."

The Sheriff spun around and stomped toward his new Model-T Ford parked on the road.

"He's lying," said Tom as the Sheriff's car kicked up dust speeding out of town on the dirt road.

Will nodded.

Helen crossed her arms. "How can you say that? He's a

20

friend of my daddy. I don't know why Sheriff Jamison is acting so strange, but he wouldn't lie."

"Sorry Helen," said Tom. "He did, and I think I know why."

"Not here," said Will. "Let's walk over to the Wright house so we can't be heard."

The three hurried along the dusty street and plopped down on the side porch of the abandoned house. It sat off the main street with woods on three sides of the dilapidated building. They needed a private place and no one ever came there.

"So, tell me," Helen demanded, her lips a thin line.

"There're only two reasons the Sheriff would lie," said Tom. "One, he's on the take. You know, somebody's paying him to keep quiet."

Helen shook her head.

"It happens," Tom said gently. "Second is that Jamison's afraid. He's been threatened. And the Deputy's death may have been a warning."

Helen's eyes widened. "But who ...? Who around here would do such a thing? We know everybody. Even the ornery Bakers wouldn't kill anyone."

"What about the new people on the hill? The Sheriff gave us the best clue. Since they bought the land and

Toothy is guarding it, they're our prime suspects."

Will snorted. "Clue? Well, now we have Tom Wallace, Private Detective. Too many books, little cuz."

Tom clenched his teeth. "Quit calling me little cuz. You're only a year older. And I can kick your butt any time."

Will shrugged.

"You two are acting like second graders," said Helen. "That does sound a little far-fetched though, Tom. This is Shakertown. Nothing ever happens here."

"But the barge showed up," said Tom, "then the Deputy died, and now there's an armed guard along the river. I got a hunch something big is happening and I'm going to find out what it is."

"Oh, shit," said Will grinning at Helen. "We're in trouble now."

CHAPTER
Four

The next night Will and Tom slogged through the fields towards High Bridge. The single track railroad bridge spanned the river at a height of nearly three hundred feet making it a good vantage point. Tom carried his father's spyglass in its leather case. They planned to spend most of the night on the trestle watching the river. The three quarter moon provided plenty of light.

The boys settled on a ledge below the trestle, pulling their collars up against the cool wind. They had wanted to talk about the barge, but worked in separate barns all day. Tom broke the silence. "Why would anybody haul a barge in against that cliff and leave it there? Then post a guard on the other side of the river. Who would bother that old piece of junk?"

"That's what I thought. Toothy sure looked capable of

bashing somebody's face in. But why draw attention to the barge—especially if there's something important on it?"

"What could be on that rusty thing? And why is it anchored so close to the dam? If a guy line breaks, it could go over."

"I've been pondering that," said Will. "Maybe we'll learn something tonight."

"I feel like we're in a Crow's Nest," said Tom.

"In a tree?"

"No, on a ship. Crow's Nest. Like in *Treasure Island*. You know, that place up on the mast where the pirates searched the sea. That gave me the idea to come here."

"I *don't* know. I ain't got time for all that crap. I always have chores to do."

"I had to work for Grandfather too, but after Mama died, I was by myself a lot. Books taught me stuff."

"Huh? You can't even milk a cow."

"I did."

"You spilt most of it."

"I'll learn farm stuff, too. I have to."

"Not from books."

"I could. They teach agriculture at the university."

"Takes money, pal, and you ain't got any."

Tom sighed. "Not yet anyway."

Tom thought of Shaker gold and focused the spyglass on the barge. The shadowed trees on the bank above the rusty scow limited his vision. He could make out the wheelhouse, but nothing else. Branches swayed and leaves twisted in the slight breeze.

Tom watched for an hour, switching eyes until his pupils twitched. Suddenly, he spotted shadows climbing on the barge. His heart thumped as he strained to see. Like wraiths, the figures moved on and off the old boat.

He blinked. "Take a look. I see something, but my eyes are tired."

The second the brass eyepiece reached his eye, Will jerked.

"Tom! There's something white, moving along the bank beside the barge. Doesn't look like a flashlight, maybe a candle, but it's under the trees."

"Let me look."

Tom took the spyglass as a freight train rattled across the trestle. In one quick move, Will reached down in his boot and pulled out a small .22 caliber pistol. Tom's mouth dropped open. "Where did you get that?"

Will touched Tom's arm. "Something moved in the thicket beside the tracks. Not more than twenty feet away."

Will climbed over the rocks towards the track holding

the pistol in front of him. Tom followed, pulse racing, trying to place his feet gently on the loose rock, but his left foot slipped sending a small avalanche of pebbles ricocheting down the slope. A dark form darted from the bushes and ran down the rails into the darkness.

"Let's get him," said Will.

The fleeing phantom jumped over the track and disappeared into the foliage. Tom and Will followed, branches and briars clawing at their faces. Ahead, twigs snapped and leaves crunched as the mysterious watcher charged through the brush.

Then quiet.

Panting, the boys stopped. Tom's skin tingled as the blackness enclosed them. A faraway owl gave its mournful call. Tom tensed when a small creature skittered through the underbrush. Will crouched, searching in the leaf-filtered moonlight for signs of the intruder. He found nothing.

"Looks like somebody was watching us," said Will as they retraced their steps to the trestle. "Spooked me." He let out a soft whistle.

"Why do you whistle all the time?" asked Tom.

"I don't know. Just nervousness, I guess. Bother you?"

"No, I don't care."

The boys sprawled back on the ledge. Tom tried to calm his heavy breathing.

"This whole thing is getting too weird, Will. Maybe we ought to talk to your daddy."

"Yeah, tomorrow morning."

"Where did you get the gun?"

"It's Daddy's—he lets me use it. Learned to shoot with it. I can knock the eye out of a squirrel. After the run-in with the Big Tooth, I thought we better have some protection."

Tom aimed the spyglass at the river. His head jerked toward Will.

"The barge is gone."

CHAPTER
Five

Sunlight flicked Tom's face and his eyes sprang open. He groaned. They had overslept. Will's snores echoed from the bed beside him. Neither wanted to get up. Tom closed his eyes against the sunshine knowing it was well past six, the time Aunt Bessie served breakfast. If you weren't on time, you didn't eat—her rule. And in this house, her word was the law.

The old Shaker building operated as a boardinghouse. Full of cousins and hired help. Aunt Bessie ran the place like a general with help from a few women in the village.

She sometimes gave him special privileges—because of his loss. He figured he'd get a biscuit and maybe country ham.

Tom rolled over. A coolness brushed his leg. Something was in his bed! He slung the covers off to find a snake crawling toward his head. He dove to the floor, yelling and searching for a weapon. Will snickered.

"There's a snake in my bed." Tom shouted.

Will burst into laughter.

Tom looked at him suspiciously. "Is it poisonous?"

Will guffawed. "A garter snake, can't hurt a flea."

"And you put it there?"

"Yep. I went to the outhouse while you were asleep and saw the little guy crawling in the grass. It's cold out there. Figured he'd like to be in a warm bed."

Tom's lips tightened and his fingers curled into a fist.

"Relax, it was just a joke."

"Get the creepy thing out of my bed," growled Tom.

Will grabbed the snake by its head and tossed it out the window.

Tom snarled. "Don't ever do that again."

He faced Will with fists raised and his teeth clenched.

"Don't be a sorehead. I'm on your side."

Tom dropped his fists and slung his pillow at Will.

A half hour later Tom rushed through the dew covered fields munching his cold ham and biscuits. He headed for the barn where he and James, a hired hand, would be storing hay. James's mother, Rose, cooked for Uncle Davis's family in the main house. Tom was sure that's why his uncle hired James—to get Rose's cooking.

After Tom's mother died, Rose did the cooking for his grandfather and him. When his grandfather got remarried, the Lincolns moved to the Wallace farm and lived in a one room shack near his uncle's house.

His mind wandered and his thoughts were all about last night. He and Will had taken turns watching and dozing until four in the morning, but the barge never returned.

Questions nagged at him. How did the barge disappear? How did it go through the lock?

Tom stumbled bleary-eyed into the barn not noticing James. The farm hand squatted in the loft and tossed a handful of hay on him. "Does Mr. Davis know you're late again?"

"Nope, and I don't expect anybody is going to tell him."

James laughed. "Won't be me."

"Thanks."

"That's okay, but you know I could never get away with being late. Mr. Jefferson Davis Wallace don't take too kindly to us colored folks."

Tom heard the bitterness in James's voice.

"How can you say that? He gave you and your momma a job."

"That he did, but he gets a mess of work out of us for

little pay. Come on, it's your turn in the loft and the wagon's coming."

Tom scrambled into the loft breathing the cool morning air. When the sun got higher, the barn would become a dusty oven. But this was the easier job, moving the hay from the front of the loft to the rear. James had to fork it out of the wagon and then heft it up.

As Tom worked, he pondered what James had said. The more he thought about it, he realized nobody on the farm treated James right. As the only Negro, he always got the worst jobs. And the other workers called him names. Leon Baker was the meanest, always harassing James who never mouthed back. His uncle never said anything to Leon.

Tom liked James's easy going nature never letting the insults get to him. James would lower his head and keep working. Tom couldn't do that. He got mad too easy and he'd have to punch somebody. *How did James manage to keep his anger inside him?* Someday Tom would ask. Rose was different. She spoke up and some white folks didn't like that.

By noon the wagon was empty. While waiting for the next load Tom asked, "What have you heard about the old barge on the river?"

"Nothin', other than it's hainted."

"Hainted?"

"Yeah, you know spirits, ghosts. Some folks call them haints."

"How do you know there's haints on the barge?"

"People seen 'em."

"Seen ghosts?"

"Yeah, I ain't seen anything, but some says they have. I don't believe it. Always thought there was a reason when somebody saw haints. Ain't saying I know anything, but if I was you, Mister Tom, I'd stay away from that thing."

"Why should I stay away?"

"Like I said, I ain't saying nothing. Just be careful."

"And don't call me Mister Tom. I'm not old enough."

"You're white folks."

"Yeah? So what?"

James pointed to an approaching wagon and picked up the pitchfork. "It makes a difference to lotsa white people."

Tom sweated out the rest of the day in the loft and after work met Will crossing the field from the West Lot house.

"Go get clean clothes on and meet me at Helen's," said Will. "I saw her around lunchtime and her daddy needs something from Lexington. He's going to let me drive his new car. He bought a '23 Dodge. And one of Helen's friends is coming along."

"Who?"

"Her name's Louise. Lives just out of town. I don't know if you've met her. She'll show you a good time." Will grinned.

Tom hustled to his West Lot room and sniffed his clothes. He found a shirt that smelled better than a wet dog. He washed his face and hair at the well pump and hurried to Helen's house.

Will was getting instructions from Helen's father. Tom stifled a chuckle as he watched Mr. Hardy circling the car, pointing. Will's head was nodding like a pine tree in high winds.

Tom frowned when he ended up in the back seat with Louise. He wondered whose idea it was for Louise to join them, Will's or Helen's. He figured Will had planned for him to be with Louise, but Helen must have gone along. The thought made his stomach queasy. Louise was cute with her brown hair and dancing eyes, but she was nothing like Helen.

Will didn't leave Shakertown by the Lexington Road, but drove south out of town.

"Where are you going?" Tom asked.

"Daddy wants me to drop off an order at Ashley's farm store in Danville. I'll go across Kings Mill."

"I wish we were crossing Brooklyn Bridge," said Louise. "I'd like to peek in the River Bar, but my daddy said he'd kill me if he caught me drinking in there."

"They can't serve liquor there since prohibition, can they?" asked Tom.

"Not supposed to, but everybody says they have it, or you can bring your own," said Will. "I'll stop at Nave's and get you some pop instead. Will that be close enough to booze Louise?"

Louise laughed and turned to Tom, her eyes twinkling. "What was it like living in a graveyard?"

Out of the corner of his eye Tom saw Helen glare at Louise and shake her head.

"I don't like to talk about it much," Tom said.

Louise nodded, looking confused.

She doesn't know. Probably the only person in two coun-

'is mind drifted back to his small upstairs room at
father's house where he could look out the window
ows of tombstones. His eyes always went to the
t across the road. Side by side. Two large ones and
ne with the tiny cross. He never wanted to look
tombstone, but he often found himself wander-
ıdow to stare at it.

He gazed out the car window at passing farms trying to erase the memory.

After stopping in Danville, Will pulled into Nave's Store at Camp Nelson before crossing the Kentucky River and the four piled out.

As they ambled back to the car with sodas and snacks, a powerful rumble of an engine caught Tom's ear. A large truck idled on the opposite side of the road and a figure leaned over in the cab. Tom couldn't make out the man's face, but he got a strange feeling. He looked at the others. They were laughing and talking. He glanced again at the truck and climbed in the back seat.

The car rattled across the rickety covered bridge and snaked its way up the winding road out of the river valley.

About halfway up the hill they heard the roar of an engine behind them. Tom spun around and paled. The truck. Closing on them, fast.

"Look out!" said Tom.

"Shit," said Will, as he sped up.

The truck matched their speed and eased up tapping their bumper. The girls screamed, and Tom grabbed the seat. He couldn't see the driver because of the sun's glare on the windshield. As they approached a hairpin turn, the truck suddenly accelerated and pulled alongside.

"What is that fool doing?" said Will. "If a car comes on the other side there'll be hell to pay."

Tom glanced up to see the driver grinning at him—a single-tooth grin.

"It's Toothy," bellowed Tom. "He's forcing us off the road."

A small wooden guardrail separated them from a quarter mile drop to the river. Helen gasped as she looked out the window at the cliff below.

Will stomped the brakes and locked all four wheels. He crammed the gearshift into reverse and popped the clutch as the truck veered toward them. The gears screamed and the car shuddered. It shot backwards as the mammoth vehicle swerved into their lane. The right rear of the truck clipped their left front fender and spun the car, turning it sideways in the road. It screeched to a halt.

The truck vanished around the curve.

Louise's fingers bit into Tom's arm, and he heard her soft sobs. Her body trembled against his. His hands shook, too. He put his arm around her. Nobody spoke for a long time. The sounds of sniffles and heavy breathing filled the car.

Will whistled out a breath. "That son of a bitch was trying to kill us."

"Why?" asked Helen her voice shaking.

"The barge," said Tom. "It has to have something to do with the barge. That's where we saw Toothy."

Will put the car in gear and turned down the hill back towards Shakertown.

"I'm sorry, Helen," he said. "I hope I didn't tear up your dad's gears."

"I don't think he'll care. You saved our lives."

She was looking at Will in a way Tom hadn't seen before. Tom clenched his fists at his side. He pulled Louise closer, and she snuggled against him.

They drove back over the river to see a row of cars stopped, waiting to get on the bridge.

"The road was blocked off," said Will in amazement.

"And look." Tom pointed at a white truck with official markings that pulled away from the front of the line of cars and sped toward Danville.

"Follow it," said Tom.

The girls glanced at each other with confused stares.

Tom turned to them. "They stopped traffic so no one could see Toothy and the truck murder us. They probably had somebody at the top of the hill blocking traffic too."

"That's awful," said Helen, her lips trembling.

"Yeah," said Will. "Whoever did this knew what they

were doing. Toothy must have pulled in right behind us and the white truck followed and blocked the road after we got on the bridge."

Will mashed the accelerator and the car leapt. Helen yelled, "No, let him go. We don't know who we're dealing with. They might have guns."

Will slowed down, and eyeballed Helen.

"You're right. We're way out of our league here."

"We have to talk to the Sheriff again," said Helen.

"Please don't," said Louise. "I'm not supposed to be out of Shakertown. I sneaked out. Daddy's mad cause I stayed out late last week."

"We'd be wasting our time with the Sheriff," said Tom. "He can't, or won't help us. And we might get him in trouble. For the time being let's keep this to ourselves. Just say a car clipped us on a curve and kept going."

"I don't think that's a good idea, Tom," said Helen. "This is serious, and we need to do something. How did they know we were on this road?"

An icy ball formed in the pit of Tom's stomach. "They've been watching us!"

Helen grabbed Will's arm.

Tom pounded his fist into the car seat. The girls jumped.

"We're not going to tell the Sheriff, but I'm mad and I *intend* to do something."

Three pairs of eyes locked on him.

Will said, "What?"

"I'm going to get on that barge."

CHAPTER
Six

The following morning the boys worked repairing fences. A farm hand dropped off a load of rough-cut boards, and they sawed, nailed, and whitewashed the replacement slats. Their discussions were about the barge and the truck. And how to figure out the barge's secret. The only way was to get on it, and Tom had an idea.

Will slopped paint on a board and pestered Tom about his plan. "Cough it up, if you got anything."

"I want to know about the Hardy's car first."

"I can fix the fender and the gears are okay. Helen's parents were pissed, but we told them it was only a minor accident. I'm not sure they bought it.

So tell me."

"We need a boat," said Tom.

"Oh good," said Will, "this is your big plan. A boat. I figured we'd get one of them new biplanes and fly over. I need to read more books to be as smart as you."

Tom flicked paint on him. Will grinned and slowly dipped his paintbrush into the paint can, keeping his eyes locked on Tom.

"Don't," Tom said, glaring at Will with eyes that said, "I dare you."

Will ambled over to Tom and with one quick movement slopped the brush across Tom's face including his mouth. Tom spat and jumped up. He charged Will, grabbing his legs and yanking. Will thumped down on his rump and the two wrestled, snatching at the paintbrush. Then they both fell on their backs laughing.

"We better get to the pond and wash off before Daddy sees us," said Will.

"Oh, I'm betting he's done worse. Mama told me stories about my father and yours, and how they were always in trouble as kids. Said Grandpa would take a switch to them even when they were near grown."

"You wouldn't know it by the way he acts now. Mr. Jefferson Davis Wallace, the big cheese. Hardly ever even smiles. Only Mama can get him to act like he's a human."

"He's running a big operation," said Tom. "All these farms. And it's tough times for everybody."

"Yeah, I know, and he's worried to death about the

Negroes taking over."

Tom raised up on his elbows and stared at Will. "Negroes, taking over? That makes no sense. How would they do that?"

"I don't know, but Daddy's always talking about it. And the women too now that they can vote."

Tom thought back to the times when he and James talked, and sometimes argued, about whether Negroes ought to be able to do all the things white folks could. James kept quoting the Declaration of Independence. He said Rose made him learn everything in it.

"That's crazy, but it reminds me," said Tom. "James says the colored folks think the barge is hainted. Says they've seen ghosts on it. Remember, you saw something from High Bridge."

"Ain't nothing but superstition, and all I saw was a candle."

"I'm not so sure. James doesn't believe in haints, but I think he knows more than he's telling about the barge."

"Don't tell Daddy that. It'll just give him something else to worry about."

"He better be worried about what's going on down on the river. I think the whole town's in trouble with somebody like Toothy around."

"So what's your plan? And no more Tomfoolery, come up with something better."

"We get a boat and drift down to the barge. Has to be a moonless night. You know, like when Washington crossed the Delaware in the middle of the night to attack the Hessians."

"He had an army, knot head. We don't know what's on that barge. It may be Toothy. I don't fancy meeting him on a dark night."

"The reason Washington won was surprise. The British had more soldiers and they were better trained, but the Americans hit them while they were asleep. They won't expect two boys to be on the river in the middle of the night. I want to find out what is so important that they're trying to kill us. Then we can tell somebody, like your daddy."

Will shook his head. "I got a bad feeling about this, but I know if I don't go with you, you'll go alone. And Toothy would chew you up with his one gold tooth."

Tom grinned. "Know anybody with a boat?"

"Old man Brent has a ratty rowboat he's let me use for fishing. We'll have to borrow it during the day and tell him we'll bring it back the next day. He'll probably give us some moonshine too."

"Louise wanted liquor."

"Don't give *her* moonshine. You'll wake up married."

Tom held up his hands and chuckled. "Uh, uh, I'm not marrying anybody. I'm getting out of here as quick as I can get some money."

"Where would you go?"

"Somewhere up north. Where nobody knows me and they don't know what happened at Grandfather's. And there has to be a big library. Not like the hundred-book closets we have around here."

"What about Helen?"

"What about her? She doesn't know I'm alive. She's got goo-goo eyes for you."

"I've been trying to kiss her for two years. I ain't nothing but her friend."

"I like Helen, but all I want to do is take a train out of Shakertown."

"And before you go, find out about the barge?"

"Yeah, and maybe find Shaker gold."

"Okay, there's no moon on Friday. We'll get the boat Friday morning."

The boys asked Will's father to let them off for a few hours on Friday to fish. He wondered why they couldn't wait till Saturday and Will convinced him the new moon would make the fish bite.

Early Friday as they walked to the river, the Baker house appeared in the fog. Junior Baker sat on the falling down porch, whittling. The two nodded to Junior. He jumped up and came toward them.

"Where do you think you're going?" he said.

"Fishing," said Will, holding up the poles.

"I can see that. Where?"

"On the river."

Tom laughed and the big kid reddened.

"You think you're funny, Wallace. Both you and your shrimp of a cousin."

Tom stiffened. Will put his hand on Tom's shoulder.

"And I heard the shrimp is sweet on the redheaded whore."

Tom's eyes narrowed, and Will tightened his grip on Tom.

"You're full of shit," said Will.

"I am, huh? She puts out for everybody. I know from personal experience."

Tom's fist clenched, and he strained against Will's hand.

Will grinned at Junior. "She don't, and you ain't never told the truth, Junior, but if she ever did, you'd be her last choice, right behind a hobo." He turned to Tom.

"He's stupid. Don't scuff your knuckles on him."

Junior laughed with a sneer. "The little boy couldn't hurt anything, unless it was a baby."

Tom shoved Will out of the way and charged Junior like an angry bull. His head hit the larger boy in the pit of his stomach and he went down hard with a loud "oof." Tom was on top swinging when Will dragged him off.

"Don't kill him. Daddy would be mad."

Will tugged Tom away from the boy and left Junior lying in the dust.

Tom stared at his feet. *Why did he let Junior make him mad? Stupid people would always make cracks about what happened.* He'd have to face worse in September in high school. He'd already met Alrik Swenson whose family lived in the Dix Valley. Alrik made a few remarks when Tom ran into him at the general store. He would be one of the worse. Tom didn't know if he could take the teasing. The guilt and rage overwhelmed him, and made him even more certain he had to leave Shakertown.

"Don't let that fool get to you," said Will. "If you hurt him, he'll cry to Leon, and Daddy'll come after both of us."

"Why does your dad put up with Leon?"

"Beats me. The whole family is worthless. Daddy should

have fired him years ago."

They reached the Brent house around eight in the morning. Tom had noticed the run down place before, but thought it was abandoned. The scruffy cabin sat on stilts and listed toward the river. *Obviously been flooded,* thought Tom. *How could anybody live there?* Across the river sat the barge. They didn't know when it returned.

Tom gingerly followed Will up the rotted wooden steps to the porch.

"He's probably asleep," said Will. "Watch your step on this raggedy-ass porch."

He pounded on the door. "Sometimes if he's had a little too much moonshine, he'll sleep all morning. We could just take the boat, but when Brent saw it missing he would figure that somebody stole it and call the Sheriff. Or get his shotgun and start shooting."

Will beat on the door again. A grizzled old man carrying a shotgun opened the door. His eyes were red and his white hair stuck straight up. The ragged clothes he wore looked like they hadn't been cleaned in a month, and his smell almost knocked Tom off the porch.

"What do you want?"

"Howdy, Mr. Brent," said Will. "We'd like to borrow your rowboat to do a little fishin' if that's okay."

"Shoot, I was going to go fishing today myself. Not sure I can let you have it."

"Well, if you're using it, we'll find another boat. But you remember, don't you, that I always bring fish back for you."

The old man scratched himself and spit on the porch. "Yeah, you do, and you helped me out round the house a few times. Take the boat, I'll just go tomorrow."

The door slammed.

"Well, how about that," said Will, "he never even offered us any moonshine."

"Are you sure we ought to take his boat?"

"He says that every time. The ornery guy hasn't been fishing in weeks. Probably drown himself if he did. It's a real shame about that man. Daddy says he comes from a good family. They came here from down in Clay County when the old man was a kid. Hard working folks. And Brent got good grades in school. He moved up north and everybody thought he was doing well. The rest of the family left a few years after he did and abandoned this house.

He came back two months ago and moved into it. It's falling down around him and it's been flooded several times. Moldy as all get-out. Won't let nobody in the house. I went in once to help him, but he wouldn't let me out of the living room. He drinks all the time and makes his own rot-gut.

The Sheriff don't care if he sells a bit of it. Daddy says that's what liquor'll do to you."

The boys followed the wobbly stone steps down to where the boat was tied to a tree. They'd need to haul it twenty feet or so to the river. Tom circled the boat shaking his head. Several boards had gaps between them. He wasn't sure it would even float.

"It'll work fine," said Will, "for what we're going to do. We'll probably kill ourselves going over the dam, or Toothy will shoot us. A leaky boat is the least of our worries."

Tom chuckled, and the two hoisted the boat and staggered down to the river. Tom held a rope tied to a metal hook on the front, and they pushed it out. Water immediately seeped through the cracks. Tom quirked an eyebrow.

"It'll leak a bit until the wood swells enough to seal," Will said. "We'll have to bail for a while."

"Where are we going to hide it until tonight?"

"There's a sandbar just upstream. Has a thicket of willows growing on it. We'll tie it up there. And that's a good place to fish too. We have to take fish back to Daddy and old man Brent."

Will handed Tom the oars as he sloshed through the seeping water, and Tom slipped them into the oarlocks. They took turns, one rowing, the other fishing. Will hooked a couple of smallmouth bass on the way to the sandbar. Tom managed to backlash his reel twice before they got there.

After a few hours at the sandbar and a half dozen caught catfish, they headed in. Tom unloaded the fishing equipment and the oars. Will said no one would steal a boat without oars. They planned to carry them back to Shakertown with them. Will stripped to his underwear and swam the boat out to the sand bar and tied it to a tree.

On the way back to Brent's house they noticed a Negro boy wearing only a pair of tattered shorts fishing on the bank. The boy turned toward them and waved. They recognized James. Tom lifted his hand as Will said, "I wonder why he's fishing here. Never see anybody fishing along this part of the river. Nothing but mud along the bank."

"He's been swimming too, his shorts are wet."

"Don't think so. Negroes are scared of water."

"What?"

"I don't know. That's what everybody says."

"Looks like everybody's wrong."

Will shrugged.

Tom looked back at James, who was still watching them. *Why would James be swimming by himself this time of day? And how did he get off work?* James seemed to act like he'd gotten caught at something. He had glanced toward Brent's house and then back at them.

After giving the catfish to Brent who didn't ask about the boat, they got to the farm by lunch. Will showed Tom how to clean the rest of the fish. Then the two dropped the fillets off at the West Lot house on the way to the barn to work.

Tom couldn't concentrate. All day he thought of the barge and what was on it. Had to be something important. Otherwise, why armed guards, and why would Toothy try to kill them? His chest tightened thinking about the scary man.

That night he tossed, and drifted in and out of sleep dreaming of the barge. Will shook him sometime after midnight.

At one in the morning the two boys smeared mud on their faces and swam to the sandbar. In their sopping wet clothes they scrunched in the boat. Will brought paddles he'd taken from one of his father's boats. Boats he wasn't allowed to use. Paddles would be better than oars. Oars might squeak.

As they floated, Tom glimpsed a pinpoint of light on the shore opposite the barge. Then it vanished. Will continued to paddle, apparently not noticing. *Did he imagine that?* The flash was similar to the light he saw on the barge when they found the Deputy's body. Will didn't see that one either. He shivered, and not from the slight breeze. He tried not to bump the paddle on the side of the boat. Terror gripped him as he thought what might happen if Toothy caught them. They would end up like the Deputy.

They sculled across the river and drifted toward the barge.

CHAPTER
Seven

The decrepit boat groaned as waves tapped gently against its side. The two boys dipped their paddles into the ink-stained Kentucky River while a wisp of a breeze ruffled their dark clothes.

"How much further?" murmured Tom.

"Shh, sounds carry a long way on water. Don't talk anymore than you have to. When we're closer, the sound of the falls will muffle our voices."

Tom dove to the bottom of the boat as something whizzed past his face.

"What was that?"

"A banshee," replied his cousin, his voice a whisper. "It'll rip your soul out."

"I'm not sure I have one. What the hell *was* that?"

Will leaned forward and put his mouth near Tom's ear.

"Probably a barn owl. Just looking for food. And don't worry, it ain't gonna be you. He wants something that ain't full of shit. Now be quiet. You wanted to do this. Let's not scream out we're coming."

Tom nodded. *Was this another one of his dumb ideas?* The barge was likely an empty derelict, but it seemed to be the reason for the weird happenings. Like the Sheriff lying and Toothy trying to run them off the road. He was determined to find out why.

The boys stayed near the side of the river where guy lines anchored the barge. Even with no moon, a boat in the center of the river would be a darker form against the blackness of the water. Along the bank, under the trees and cliff, they blended into the suffocating night.

The rusty hulk was a quarter-mile downstream. They drifted toward it. The fifteen foot high rock dam spanned the river at the lock, forming a pool deep enough for large boats and barges. Eddies swirled, and the speed of the water intensified near the dam. They didn't want to get too close. The sound of the water pouring over the dam muffled the calls of night birds.

Tom strained his eyes searching for the moored barge that sat a stone's throw from the dam. His breath came in quick gasps. This was another crazy thing to do. Maybe Will was right—he did have a death wish. But he didn't want to die, he wanted to forget.

Will leaned closer to Tom and whispered. "Go easy now. We don't want to run right into that piece of junk."

"Do you see it?" asked Tom.

"Don't see nothing."

They floated, the blackness draping them like a shroud. A twig popped and rocks rattled on the bank less than six feet away. Both boys jumped.

"Something's up there, something big," said Tom.

"Nah, probably raccoon or—" started Will.

A wood-splintering crash in the center of the boat interrupted him. Water poured in and the boat foundered.

"What the...?" said Tom.

"Somebody tossed a boulder."

"Toothy."

The boat sank up to the gunwales soaking both boys to the waist.

"Quick, in the water," said Will. "Swim the boat up-stream."

Tom rolled into the murky river. His heart pounded. He strained, pulling with one hand and paddling with the other. They made no headway. The current flowing over the dam had already gripped the boat and it was too full of water to move against the current.

"What now?" cried Tom. "Swim to shore?"

"Not up there where that rock came from. Just hang on. We'll get on the barge."

"Bad idea," said Tom. "How about across the river?"

"Too far. The current would grab us this close to the dam. We'd never make it."

The boys drifted with the nearly submerged boat as the current tugged them toward the dam. A dark shadow appeared.

"The barge," whispered Tom. As they came alongside the darkened boat, they noticed two pinpoints of light. Cigarettes.

"Shit," said Will. "We can't get on the barge and it's too late to swim back." His voice cracked. "Get on top of the boat. Lay flat. We'll ride it over the dam."

Tom climbed back in, his stomach in knots. The river below the dam was filled with rocks. *Why had he put Will in danger?*

They stretched out, hands holding the gunwales with their feet hooked over the seats. The boat accelerated as the roar of the falls echoed in their ears. Tom's arms quivered from the tight grip and the rest of his body from fear. He strained to keep his head above the raging water. As it hit the dam, the boat succumbed to the thrashing deluge and cracked down the center.

The boys careened over the dam.

CHAPTER
Eight

The momentum of the boat and the rushing water catapulted the two boys away from the fang-toothed rocks below the dam. They swam with the current downstream to a sand bar and crawled on the damp sand. Their gasps sounded in the darkness.

"You okay?" whispered Will. Tom didn't answer. Only the sound of a whippoorwill filled the night air.

"Hey," said Will in a louder voice. "Are you okay?"

"No."

"What's the matter?"

"I'm dead."

"Quit goofing around. You scared me half to death."

"That's good, cause you're dead too."

"Did you hit your head on a rock coming over the falls?"

"No, I got an idea."

"Not again. What are we going to do this time? Leap off of High Bridge to see if we can fly."

"Be quiet, I'm trying to think."

"That scares me too."

"Have you ever read Huckleberry Finn?"

"I've told you before I gotta work. Ain't got time for reading."

Tom ignored his comment. "In the book Huck and Jim, the runaway slave, have an accident and people think they're dead. If you're dead you can do things because people aren't expecting you to be around. As of right now we're dead."

"Sorry, pal, I'm not going to do that to my mother."

"What about your dad?"

"Yeah, he'd be real upset about losing two unpaid hired hands."

Tom chuckled softly in the darkness.

"Okay what about me? I'm dead."

"Why do you want to do this? Let's give it up. Somebody else can figure out the barge."

"I'm not sure why. Farm work's boring and I need excitement. And it helps me forget, at least for a while."

"Then let's go back to hunting gold. Finding that would be exciting."

"We don't have any idea where to look and just hiking

around's no fun."

"So excitement for you is nearly getting killed?"

"No, there's the mystery too. I'm going to do this, with or without you."

Will didn't answer for a moment. "I don't know, I still don't think it's a good idea. How are you going to get away with it?"

"Well, nobody gives a rat's rump about me anyway, so it's not going to be a big deal. And that will give me a chance to snoop around."

"You're the biggest fool in the county. What about Helen? And Aunt Bessie, and my mama? They care about you. You haven't thought this out. Where you going to stay and what are you going to eat?"

"I'll be busy saving the hides of all the useless people in Shakertown. You have to get me food."

"I reckon with an attitude like that you're going to be awfully hungry."

"The hell with you then. I'll figure something out."

"Calm down. I won't let you starve. You could ask nicely though."

"Sorry," said Tom.

He hesitated and slumped his shoulders.

"I'm scared, Will. I know your family cares about me.

They took me in. But this is the second time Toothy tried to kill us. And I'm afraid for your folks and Helen's. I don't know what we're dealing with here, but these people will do anything."

"Yeah," said Will in a raspy voice. "I'm scared too. They'd hunt us down like an egg-stealing fox. And, other than Toothy, we don't know who any of them are. Toothy is bad enough, I'd hate to run into the others. But one of these days, I'm going to repay that big ox for that crap on the Lexington Road."

He was quiet for a moment.

"Okay, this makes me nervous—again, but I don't know what else to do. Nobody would believe us. I'd better get home and think up a story on the way. It's got to be a good one."

"If anybody can, it'll be you," said Tom.

"I'll float downstream and scratch myself up more. Make it look serious. I'll meet you back here tomorrow evening. There's good cover here. Be careful. Toothy don't know you're dead yet, so he might try to kill you again. And watch out for snakes."

Tom swallowed the lump that rose in his throat. Now what was he getting himself into? He hadn't thought about snakes in the rocks.

The boys separated. Will drifted downstream and Tom eased back into the turbid water. He fought the current to the side of the river where the barge was tethered, hauled himself up on the muddy goo, and plodded upstream.

The night was as black as one of Aunt Bessie's cast iron skillets. The only sounds were the drones of frogs and crickets and the distant roar of the dam.

After an hour of walking, and clambering over rocks, Tom passed the abandoned lockmaster's house at the dam. The sound of falling water would cover his noise now.

Tom crawled and slithered through mud and brambles at the edge of the dam. He heaved himself over downed logs as critters skittered in the underbrush. Then the dark hulk of the barge appeared. It came upon him quick, and he ducked behind a log.

No one moved anywhere around the floating wreck. He lay still, planning to stay near the barge over night and through the next day. But he'd have to find good cover.

Mosquitoes feasted on his bare flesh and a water snake splashed softly into the current. Bats zigzagged across the night sky. *Not nearly enough of them. They needed to be down here eating these mosquitoes.*

He flattened as noise came from the barge and something splashed in the river. The darkness prevented him from seeing anything, but voices murmured above the water's roar. The din of the dam kept him from making out what they were saying.

He debated whether to go closer. It would be another stupid thing to do. Stupid and dangerous. He'd barely avoided being killed twice already. He should stay put, but after coming this far he had to learn something.

Tom wormed his way through a forest of jagged rocks hoping he didn't wake a den of copperheads. He neared the barge and the glow of cigarettes let him make out silhouettes leaning against the deck railing. The whispers of the men's voices added to the night sounds.

As Tom crept, his hand hit the river water causing a splash. The figures on the barge turned and one said. "What the ...?"

Another man responded, "Ain't nothing. Probably a frog."

Tom lay still, barely breathing. When the men went back to their conversation, he edged along the bank until he could have touched the barge with a stick. He laid alongside the river in stinking mud.

He strained to hear the voices when a twig popped to his side. He slowly turned his head and sucked in his breath. A white apparition glowing in the dark moved near him. His mouth went dry as he watched the ghostlike figure drift toward him, its form billowing in the night air. Tom wanted to run or burrow into the earth.

It was James's haint.

CHAPTER
Nine

Tom had nowhere to go. He lay quiet, hoping the pounding of his heart wouldn't start an avalanche on the cliffs above. As the apparition neared him, he discovered it wore work boots. His eyes locked on a man covered in white muslin holding a candle lantern under the cloth. Tom's muscles relaxed and he breathed again. James's haint was no ghost after all.

The sheet-covered man appeared to float as he moved along the bank. Apparently making a circle with the idea to scare off any one curious enough to try to get close to the barge. If someone did, then Toothy would take over. His throat tightened as he remembered the look in the man's eyes.

His ears strained to catch the voices over the thundering of the waterfall. He got snatches of conversation. "Next week." He heard surprised murmurs as one of the men said, "the boss man."

Two guards left the barge and walked toward the palisade cliff. Tom's head filled with questions as the dim figures faded into the cliff's shadow. *Almost like they vanished inside the rock face. Did they go into a cave?*

The palisades rose two hundred feet above the river. Caves and crevices honeycombed the hillsides. He had hiked along the top of the bluffs once and seeing the drop to the river tightened his stomach.

An idea swirled in his mind. A hunch he'd share with Will tomorrow, but in the meantime he wanted to learn the purpose of the barge. He needed a vantage point. Some place to hide during the day and watch. Maybe find out if the two men did go into a cave.

He crawled into the rocks at the face of the cliff. This spot was opposite the dam so he wasn't too worried about making noise. The river drowned out any sounds he made. Although he couldn't be completely sure if a guard below the falls might hear him.

As he picked his way through rocks and boulders, he thought of Will's caution on snakes. Will had taught him about the ones along the river. Copperheads were the most prevalent throughout the Palisades. They rarely attacked and even if one bit him he probably would only get sick. Rattlesnakes were worse—much more aggressive, bigger, and their bite produced more poison. They usually gave a warning, but if Tom crawled over one, it would attack without rattling. The worst snake was the cottonmouth, but those snakes normally lived in swampy areas in the river bends. He was trying to discover the barge's secret, and had no choice but to hope he didn't wiggle over a snake.

He stumbled upon a cove surrounded by rocks with a gap between two of the larger boulders. He could see the barge from here, but anyone on it couldn't spot him. He spent the rest of the night dozing and watching. The pops and cracks of twigs told him guards patrolled below the dam. He estimated there were at least four, two on the barge, and two walking around. A total of five counting the haint. Tom squirmed in the sticks and leaves trying to find a comfortable place to sleep. Fatigue finally took over and he drifted off.

Tom didn't wake until after daybreak when the sun glistened on the river in a dance of crystal. He berated himself for sleeping late, but the sound of the falls muffled all noise, and he was exhausted. He peeked through the opening at the barge. No sign of movement anywhere. He searched for an opening in the cliff face near where the two men disappeared. Large boulders in the area in front of the barge blocked his vision. He checked below the dam and saw nothing but the swirling river and the spring-green of the trees along the bank. Everything seemed peaceful. But he knew better.

Tom kept his eye on the barge throughout the day and no guard, or anyone else, went near it. He assumed men were still on the scow. They probably worked all night and slept in daytime, but someone must be keeping an eye out for intruders. He scanned the hillside without locating any watchers. At one point he did glimpse a shadow move on the bank by the water, but he couldn't make out what it was. Maybe an animal, a mink or a beaver.

Several broken bottles scattered in the mud near the barge caught his eye. They appeared to be all the same shape and size. They helped to confirm his hunch about the barge. The thought came from stories he'd read in the news. It seemed a bit far-fetched though, for a small town in Kentucky.

The sun drifted below the hills and he got ready to meet Will. This would be the most dangerous time. When he left his shelter he'd be exposed and the guards, wherever they were, might discover him. He didn't know what else to do. If he waited till dark Will would be concerned and come looking for him, not knowing that guards stalked the area. He realized that it was only dumb luck that allowed him to crawl from below the dam to the barge without running into a guard.

Tom decided to stay in the rocks against the cliff hoping that the watchers were above him. He hadn't seen any movement on the barge, although guards might watch through peepholes from inside the scow. He wasn't worried about being quiet, he was worried about being spotted.

Tom left his hiding spot at dusk. He thought how they should have been smarter and set a time to meet after dark so he wouldn't be exposed. The cool mud seeped into his pants as he crawled, trying to keep rocks and trees between him and the barge.

The bank sloped following the downhill flow of the river and once he got below the falls, he'd be out of sight of anyone on the barge. However, if guards roosted in the cliffs, they'd spot him. Tom eased his way through the boulders and downed logs staying low to the ground and keeping his eyes open for snakes. He'd squirmed a hundred yards past the dam before he felt safe from the men on the barge. He still hesitated to stand, and slithered through slimy mud while crossing a small stream. An idea formed— the muck could camouflage him. Tom smeared mud all over his arms and head and wiggled around in the mud puddle. And crawled some more. With his head and face completely covered with brown gook, he thought he might look like a log in the river. Tom slipped into the water and floated with the current.

The sandbar came into view and he paddled toward it. His stomach growled, sounding like a bear underwater. He hoped Will managed to get some of Aunt Bessie's fried chicken. His body relaxed for the first time in a day as he swam toward the refuge to eat and rest. Then his arm stopped in mid stroke and a shudder swept his body. A rowboat swung around from behind the bar and traveled directly toward him. Icy terror filled him as he saw a large man in the front of the boat, a single gold tooth sparkling in the fading light.

CHAPTER
Ten

Tom swam as silently as a water snake into a clump of reeds along the bank. If Toothy spotted him, he had no way to escape, and the man would show no mercy. Tom wasn't sure why he was so afraid of the giant. The fear sprang from more than the incident on the Lexington Road. Maybe it was the look in the huge man's eyes both times Tom had seen him. Toothy and the other man in the rowboat would kill him. He was sure. After all, he was already dead.

He tried not to move or breathe as the boat approached the reeds, hoping his mud-caked head looked like a log. Something splashed in the water beside him.

"Damn," came a voice. "I threw it in the weeds."

Tom saw a bass bait floating beside him. It jerked forward and the hooks caught on a plant.

"I'm hung up."

"Don't break the line, I'll paddle over." Tom recognized Toothy's voice.

The hairs on the back of Tom's neck prickled. If they paddled to the reeds, Tom would end up like a fish gutted on the bottom of their boat.

The fishing line was taut with the bait straining against the reeds. Tom eased the plant off the hooks and the bait jerked back toward the boat nearly hitting Toothy.

"Hey," the big man said. "You almost hooked me with that thing."

The oarlocks creaked as the boat rowed away. Tom's breath rushed out like a steam engine pulling into a station. Tom waited until the boat was out of sight and resumed swimming to the sandbar. He kept his eyes open for other boats. These people, whoever they were, patrolled the river, too. He reached the backside of the sandbar and dragged himself onto the sand. He crept through bark-stripped logs and weeds until Will whispered, "Over here."

Tom squinted and found Will perched on a log surrounded by a thicket of cattails. Will smirked. "You're about the strangest thing I've ever seen."

"I imagine I am. I thought covering myself with mud might make me harder to see."

"Yeah, what a great idea. You'd look like a little skinny

bear as you walked down the river bank."

"No, goof head. I crawled all the way from the barge to right above the sandbar. At night they got guards everywhere. I didn't see any during the day, but I know they're hiding—and watching. But I did see Toothy."

Will's eyes widened.

"Yeah," continued Tom. "In a boat. Patrolling the river. He nearly caught me, too."

Will whistled. "We're in deep shit, little cuz."

"I know, what's going on in Shakertown?"

"About what?"

"About my death, you fool."

"Ain't much of a big deal," said Will with a smug look.

"I halfway believe you. But I figure there must be somebody in the village that is sorry to hear I'm dead."

"Yeah, I'm lying. The whole place is in an uproar. Helen is beside herself. Brent even seemed concerned. Said he didn't care about the boat. And, believe it or not, Daddy is really upset. Probably more than if it was me that drowned. Threatened to beat me within an inch of my life, but Moma wouldn't let him. I wish we'd gone to him before like we planned. He thought all this was my idea and blamed me for killing you."

Tom choked. He understood blame.

"Did Helen cry?"

"Yeah, what do you think? For some strange reason she kinda likes you."

Tom's mud-packed face cracked a grin. "What did you say happened?"

"I told them we wanted to take a peek at the barge, but got too close to the dam and our boat went over. Said I couldn't find you. I looked for hours, but figured you must have been washed downstream. They sent out a search party. The Sheriff talked to me for a couple hours. He's scared shitless. He knows I'm lying, but he's afraid to find out what really happened. You're even more trouble dead than you were alive."

"Glad to hear it. Wish I could figure out a way to make real trouble for those people on the barge. I didn't find out a lot, but something important is coming. I heard them mention 'the boss man.' Don't have any idea who, or why. But I'm going to keep watching. Did you bring food? My stomach thinks my throat's been cut."

Will reached behind the log and pulled out a sack.

"I scavenged what I could from every meal and then went to the store and got a couple of apples and some dried meat. Ought to hold you for a while."

Tom grabbed the bag. "It's all wet."

"Well, yeah, shitface. I had to swim over. I ain't a bird dog. I couldn't carry it in my mouth."

"I'm glad you didn't. Your slobber would kill me."

Will laughed and Tom took a bite out of the soggy chicken. Tom ate while Will told more of the search for his body and how the death had the village in an uproar. Folks pondered why the Deputy died, and now Tom. People murmured about the barge. They were afraid. Rumors swirled that something was happening at the McAllen house across the river, but no one said anything out loud. Only in whispers.

Tom burped. "Thanks for the food, Will. Lying in my hiding place all day I heard my stomach growling. If it wasn't for the dam, I figured the goons on the barge would hear me. Thought I might have to start eating grubs."

"What happened to your arm? Looks like you got the chickenpox."

"Mosquitoes. Think I lost half a pint of blood overnight."

"You just laid there and let them chew on you?"

"Yeah, I couldn't slap them. Afraid somebody might hear me. After a while I didn't pay too much attention."

"You're a lot tougher than I thought for a city boy."

Tom grinned. "You may not want to hear this, but I

have another plan."

Will put his head in his hands. "I can't stand it. You'd think after someone tried to kill you—twice, you'd figure out that maybe you should stay away from those people. At least, that's what a sane person would think."

"I never claim to be sane. Do you want to hear or not?"

"Spit it out."

"I'm going to try again to get on that piece of junk and find out what's really there."

Will's jaw dropped. "After what happened? No, you're not. And I ain't going to go with you. Of all the fool things you come up with this one has to be the worst. You really are nuts. Those goons are trying to kill us. We need to get away from them not go into their lair. And just how do you expect to do this?"

"I don't know yet."

"What are you planning to do? Go to the library and check out a book that tells you how to crawl into a den of murdering thugs and get yourself killed?"

Tom rolled his eyes. "You ought to try reading a book rather than being a smart-ass. Then you might actually be smart."

Will snorted. "Even if we do this, which we're not, what do you expect to find?"

"There's a connection between the barge and the McAllen house. The Sheriff told us about the new people there and I think they're the ones using the barge. I couldn't see anything to prove that, but I got a gut feeling. I'll spend a few more days watching and maybe I can figure something out."

"You can't let this go on too much longer. People will be even more upset if they don't find your body. And sooner or later we've got to tell someone about this. About the barge I mean."

"Yeah, but right now we don't know enough to tell. Let me find out more."

CHAPTER
Eleven

Tom stuffed chicken in his pocket, and the boys separated. He swam to the bank and waited until complete darkness. Then spent an hour sneaking back to his vantage point close to the cliffs. He dozed through the night and spied the following day. Still nothing going on.

The next night brought the sounds of the guards and new voices. The tar-black sky kept him from seeing all the activity, but the barge filled with movement. He needed to get closer, but too many people milled about on the bank. More than before. Once or twice, he heard a soft clunk of what sounded like bottles hitting the ground. Cursing always followed the noise. *Were these the same as the broken ones he saw in the daylight?* That would make sense if his hunch was right. Shadowy figures paraded on and off the rusty scow. Some entered the barge by a gangplank at the center of the boat near the wheelhouse, but not all. The barge must have another entrance.

Tom lay on his belly looking through the crack in the rock and seething. He wanted to know more. Maybe the whole idea was a waste of time. The barge and its men were not going to give up their secrets easily. Then, the muffled sound of an engine filled the air above the roar of the falls. He stared and realized the barge was moving. He couldn't get closer because phantom-like figures still moved along the sandy shore. And the haint prowled.

Bright stars gave him enough light to make out the activity as the barge settled into the lock. Men on the bank controlled it with ropes tied to a railing running the length of the boat. The pumps chugged as the barge was lowered to the level of the river below the dam. He could barely hear the noise of the pumps. He realized the sound of the machinery had been muted, but the lock definitely worked. The pumps stopped and the dark shape of the ramshackle boat vanished into the night. The men disappeared, and quiet returned. Tom's eyes drifted shut.

The noise of the pumps woke Tom before daybreak as the barge reappeared. He figured it had been gone four or five hours. Men jumped off the boat and quickly tied the guy lines. They vanished back into the barge. Tom knew the barge had delivered its cargo.

Tom stayed two more days, taking breaks to meet Will for food. They speculated again about the barge's destination and its cargo. Why would outsiders come to Shakertown? They talked about Tom's hunch. The idea made sense, but was hard to believe.

Will tried to persuade Tom to quit, but he wasn't ready. Exhaustion wore on him, but he had hope something would turn up. He didn't know why learning the truth about the barge was so important to him. Yeah, Toothy almost killed him, but it was more than that. A torment gnawed at him. Maybe he wanted to be a hero, to make people forget his past. Or the excitement—where he could be lost in danger and not remember that Sunday morning. Whatever the reason, it drove him to find out.

He promised Will he'd stay only another day and then return to Shakertown. He feared what awaited him. Will had mentioned coming up with a con, but they might as well tell the truth. Uncle Davis would kick him out of the West Lot house, and the Sheriff might arrest him. And Helen ... he dreaded the thought of seeing her.

The next morning Tom awoke in his hiding place to a distant boom echoing along the river. For a moment he thought, like in *Huckleberry Finn*, somebody had fired a cannon into the river to force his body up from the bottom. He chuckled to himself. Shakertown had no cannon, and they wouldn't be searching for *him* anyway. Sure, his death stirred up the village. But if he disappeared nobody would care, except Helen and Will. A month from now, he'd be forgotten.

Another boom, and he realized a thunderstorm was drifting into the valley. The sky began to growl and the ground quaked. The first drops of rain kicked up dust around him and hit the back of his neck. The trickle turned to a deluge and lightning spider-webbed across the sky.

A sudden crack and flash seared his eyes and ears. The strike hit above him and his nose wrinkled at the acrid smell. From the cliff, a cedar tree and rocks tumbled down, crashing into the barge. The constant lightning provided enough light for Tom to see men pour out of the wheel-house to check the barge. A hatch, nearly invisible on the aft deck, opened. A head appeared and stared into the darkness. The hatch shut again.

Dumbfounded, Tom gawked as more men appeared, but not from the barge. He couldn't tell where they came from. They seamlessly worked together to remove the rocks and branches. The barge seemed to have no damage and most of the men went back in through the wheelhouse.

Several others, however, turned and walked toward a line of boulders and trees, and disappeared.

Tom grinned. Seeing the men vanish into the rock face again meant he guessed right—a cave. His pulse quickened. The days of boredom and misery had paid off. To get the whole story he had to do one more thing. And now he knew how. He only had to convince Will.

Tom rose before dawn and reached the sandbar as a thin sliver of salmon-pink sky lighted his way. He spent the day hiding, waiting for Will.

Will finally moseyed through the weeds.

"Hey, little cuz, still alive? Snakes ain't ate you yet?"

"Haven't seen a one and no tooth-man either."

"Glad to hear it. What's the news?"

Tom explained what happened and told Will his plan to get on the barge. Will groaned and shook his head.

"Remember how strong the current is there."

"How could I forget? But there's a railing that runs the length of the barge. We'll grab the railing at the stern before we get to the fast water."

Will's shoulders dropped in resignation. "Okay, we'll try it, and I think you're right about the cave, but something is missing."

Tom cocked his head.

"Why would they pick a cave next to a dam and near a town? There's caves all up and down the Kentucky River. Some so isolated they've never been explored. Why there?"

"The McAllen house," said Tom. "Must be that. We've thought the new people up there were behind this. How close is the house to the barge? You can't see it from the river."

Will thought a moment. "Right above it."

Tom jumped up. "A tunnel. There's a tunnel through the rock up to the house."

"No, it's a couple of hundred feet up. It'd be a hellava job to build a tunnel through all that rock. Something like that couldn't be hidden from the town."

"A ladder?"

"That's stupid. People would see a ladder and they couldn't load stuff. There's no way ..." Will hesitated. He slapped his forehead and his eyes locked on the upstream palisades.

"What?" asked Tom.

"There was an old Negro man that lived in town. He's dead now. But he told a bunch of us kids a story about his father, a slave. I forgot about it. Didn't mean much to kids. The man said his father escaped to the North by floating down the river. He climbed steps through a tunnel to an old mansion on a hill. The father stayed in the house until a hay wagon came and carried him and some others to Ohio. He couldn't remember where on the river, but thought it was close to Shakertown. Said the Shakers fed him."

Tom's thoughts drifted to the books he had read on the Underground Railroad. Where the slaves had escaped to the North by following the "drinking gourd," the North Star. They were helped by abolitionists along the way. And many of the stories dealt with caves and tunnels.

Tom pumped his fist into his hand. "That has to be it. There's a stairway to the house through a tunnel."

CHAPTER
Twelve

"Whoa, don't jump to conclusions," said Will. "The old man said his father traveled in darkness and didn't know where he went into the tunnel. Could have been twenty miles from here."

Tom grinned. "You don't believe that, do you?"

Will shook his head. "I'm just afraid of what you're going to do."

"We got no choice."

"There's got to be a better way," said Will.

"There isn't."

Will sighed.

Tom knew Will didn't want to try to search the barge again, but that was the only way to learn its secrets. The two finally agreed that they needed to have something conclusive before they told the village the truth about Tom. By lying, Will got himself in as much trouble as Tom. And that was the reason Will agreed.

The boys waited until dusk and swam to shore. They had decided to go back to the Wright house since the surrounding woods gave them cover.

As they walked, Tom asked, "What's it like inside?"

"Dusty and junky. I was only in it once. Scrounging around for something to sell. Ain't nothing left worth shit. Just some ratty-ass furniture."

"Any place to sleep?"

"Yeah, an old couch. You'll have to beat the dust off it. I'll bring you some blankets."

"And food?"

"Damn, I've been feeding you for days now. I didn't know dead people could eat so much."

Tom laughed. "Won't be long now until I'm back in Aunt Bessie's kitchen. I've dreamed about hot fried chicken and soup beans."

"Tonight then?" asked Will.

"Yeah, no moon and clouds. After we find out what's on the barge we can come back here and figure out what to do next."

The dark form of the Wright house appeared at the edge of the trees. Tom hadn't paid much attention to the run-down building when they had walked by or sat on the porch. But if any house ought to be haunted, it was this one. Weeds and bushes grew up in the front, and small trees sprouted throughout the yard. The shutters, what few remained, were hanging on the side of the windows, and a hole gaped in the roof where one of the chimneys had fallen. Formed of white granite from the river cliffs, it stood two stories tall with a cupola on top. The front had two doors, one for women and one for men.

The boys edged from the trees to the rear of the house. Animals, or something, had been going to the house, but not to the front door. Will said he had never got in that door—it was always locked—but once managed to open the side door. They followed a path around to the side door. A new-looking padlock anchored a board across the door, and the first floor windows were boarded up.

"Damn," Will groused. "Let's try the back."

They retraced their steps and Will pointed to the second story. A few of the upstairs windows didn't have boards sealing them. A fallen tree rested against the side of the single-story addition to the house. The tree had crushed the rear part of the wooden structure, but the edge of the roof remained solid.

"I think we can climb the trunk and get in a second-story window," said Will.

"Let's do it," said Tom.

Will jumped up on the tree and immediately fell off. Tom started up.

"Watch out," said Will. "That's as slippery as a pig in a mud hole. There ain't no bark on it and it's covered with dew."

Tom crawled the length of the tree and gently stepped onto the roof.

"Careful," said Will. "The tree busted up the roof. Stay close to the edge; it'll be stronger there."

The sky was darker now and Tom eased along the edge. He found the rafters and inched up one until he could get to a window. Will followed. The window wasn't locked, but barely moved when they pushed. Together they strained against the sill and the window creaked open. They skinnied through and stepped into an empty room.

Lung choking dust filled the house and the smell of decayed cloth stung their noses. They snuck downstairs to the room that had the couch Will had mentioned. Scattered around the space, other furniture lay in broken heaps. Tom grimaced, but thought the place could be livable with a little cleaning. He noticed footprints in the grime and trash thrown in a corner. Someone else had once used the house. Probably the people who placed the lock on the side door. He'd have to secure the upstairs windows. One of the chairs braced against the side door would keep out whoever locked it.

"Hang on little cuz," said Will. "I'll be back with your blankets and food."

Tom settled in, straightening the room and concentrating on his idea. He kept an eye on the upstairs windows, watching the weather. The now black sky showed no glimmer of a star. Perfect, thought Tom, not only a new moon, but clouds too.

Will returned after midnight lugging a bulging sack. Food and blankets for Tom, and supplies for the attempt to board the barge. Will had brought a hack saw and cut the shank of the padlock. Now they could use the side door. They would replace the lock when they left, and unless someone looked closely, they'd never notice the lock was cut. After waiting an hour, to talk through the plan, they took their gear and crept out of town.

The boys hiked Shaker Landing Road and went past the Brent house. The sandbar would be their starting point again, but this time without a boat. Will had brought a small hand saw and cut down a couple of limbs from nearby trees. Tom planned to drift down the river submerged in the midst of what they hoped looked like fallen branches. They stripped and wrapped their clothes in oil skins to keep them dry and to help them float. They tied the ends of the oil skins with short pieces of rope and looped them around their necks. They eased into the water. The stream felt cool, not cold, but Tom shivered. If they messed up he really might end up dead.

The two goose-bumped boys pushed off from the bank and into the river current. They swam silently as rain began to fall. The sound of the waterfall echoed in the distance, and the darkened barge appeared in the gloom. The soft light of a cigarette glowed on the bank. A guard. As they came alongside, they released the branches and grabbed the railing. The current tugged at them as they inched their way along the hull toward the stern. Tom tensed as they passed the wheelhouse knowing they had to be especially quiet here. They reached the stern and strained to hold on against the pull of the falls. Tom's plan was to go in the barge through the hatch he had seen during the thunderstorm.

Will gripped the railing with one hand and held Tom's clothes while Tom scrambled up the derelict, scraping himself on the rusty metal. He leaned over and took the clothes and Will joined him. Even though their eyes were accustomed to the dark, they couldn't make out anything more than two feet in front of them. Tom hoped they wouldn't walk right into a guard. He dropped and crawled on the slippery deck. Rain pattered on the rough metal as Tom felt for the hatch. He crisscrossed the deck, dreading that he might put his hand on somebody's boot. His ears pricked as he listened for a footstep.

Finally, his fingers scraped an indentation and a metal ring. He reached back and touched Will and the two grasped the ring. They cracked open the hatch. Nothing but darkness. Tom was gambling that this part of the barge was unused. During the lightning storm all the activity was near the wheelhouse.

Tom had stowed a flashlight in his clothes, but couldn't use it until they were inside with the hatch closed. Will held the round door open and Tom dangled his feet until he found the rungs of a ladder. Silence surrounded him and his muscles tightened.

Tom whispered, "Come on."

Will joined him on the ladder after closing the hatch behind him. Tom dug through his clothes and got the flashlight. He held his shirt over the light before turning it on so it released a dim glow. Around them were boxes, tables, and chairs. The galley. Tom worked the flashlight out of the cloth and searched the room. One door led to the rest of the barge. They pulled on their clothes.

Tom snapped off his light and cracked open the door. Snores and heavy breathing greeted their ears. He quickly shut the door.

"Now what?" whispered Will.

"We don't have any choice; we have to go through there. It's dark, and they're probably used to people coming and going. They'll never notice us."

Will shook his head and sighed. "You not only love going into the lion's den, you want to stick your head in his mouth."

"Yeah sure. I'm scared, but I'm mad, too. I want to get to the bottom of this. Let's wait a bit to let our eyes readjust to the darkness."

Ten minutes later they opened the door and crept into the room full of sour sweat and snores. Tom led, but couldn't see further than his hand stretched in front of him. His fingers touched hair as he stumbled into a man getting into a bunk.

"Ow," the man said. "Watch where you're going."

"Sorry," mumbled Tom trying not to let the man hear the fear in his voice. He eased past, trembling so hard he was afraid the man could feel the vibrations. His throat tightened and he tried not to gasp for breath.

Tom touched a door knob to his left and cracked the door open. He quickly shut it, gagging. The room reeked worse than any outhouse. The barge's bathroom. Probably just a bucket on the floor.

Will cleared his throat and his hand pulled Tom's shirt. Will had plowed into a smelly, hanging cloth used to block the light from the rest of the barge. Both boys held their breath trying not to cough. They peeked around it. A dimly lit corridor stretched in front of them. At the end of the passageway, metal stairs went up and down to closed doors. They inched their way glancing furtively in all directions. At the stairs Tom whispered to Will, "I bet these go up to the wheelhouse. I think they have guards in there at night. Let's go down."

Will nodded, and they cautiously placed one foot at a time on the steps. The first door was a watertight hatch with six lever-style latches holding it shut. Tom remembered reading that latches on ship doors were called dogs. They released the latches and cracked open the door. Blackness challenged them. Tom shined his light into what looked like a storage area. The boys climbed through the hatch and closed it behind them.

They snuck down the metal staircase into the darkened hole. Tom led with his flashlight, his stomach churning.

Will hung back to make sure nobody followed. This part of the barge had been divided into compartments and gave no sign of being a derelict. The paint gleamed and the steps appeared new. When they reached the floor, Tom played his light around the room. Tools hung on the walls, and boxes littered one corner.

Tom wrinkled up his nose. "What's the smell?"

"Yeah, I smell it too. Don't know."

Tom walked over to a door in the outside of the hull. It was twice the size of any other hatch they'd seen and was dogged down. He released the latches and cracked it open. Rain splashed in. The river bank appeared in the darkness and the river was less than two feet below the door.

"Why is there a door here? Barely above the river."

"Makes no sense," said Will. "Hey, look at this."

He pointed to an eight foot long plank.

"Looks like a gangway."

Will nodded. "For loading or unloading something through that outside door, and I think your hunch is right."

"Maybe. Definitely something illegal," Tom said. "I bet this barge is junky only on the outside. If we sneak around more, I know we would find that all the engines and equipment are brand new. When we were on High Bridge and it disappeared, it took a load somewhere."

"Or got something?"

"Yeah, could be that too."

The creak of a hinge interrupted Tom. He switched off his light. Someone had opened the hatch above them.

They were trapped.

Chapter
Thirteen

Will grabbed Tom's arm and pulled him to the hatch leading to the outside.

Their hands quivered as they struggled to release the dogs. Footsteps on the stairs came closer. Will gently eased the door open trying to prevent the hinges creaking. Waves slapped the side of the boat as they lowered themselves out of the opening and quickly closed the latches. They shivered standing in waist deep water between the barge and shore.

"Let's find the stairway," whispered Tom.

"Forget it. It's too dangerous now. We need to swim back across the river."

"Why don't we look around first? I'd like to know what that outside door is for and know for sure there's a stairway."

"They'll figure out somebody was in there," said Will.

"We better get out of here."

"They'll never notice anything. Too many people coming and going. We're okay."

Tom sloshed up on the bank and dropped to all fours. He felt around in the darkness while Will hesitated—waiting in the rain-chilled water. Tom's hand touched smooth rock, and he hissed at Will.

Will waded over and crouched beside Tom. The two followed a rocky path searching for a step, or some indication of the tunnel. Under the cliff and trees the blackness engulfed them. They were afraid to use flashlights because of the patrolling guards.

Tom's mouth went dry as he frantically crawled. At any moment someone might come down the tunnel and trip over them.

His knuckles banged stone and his hands groped the right angle of rock. A step. Will, now crawling beside him, whispered, "I guess you want to see where they go." Tom chuckled softly. The two moved up the steps that led between a series of large boulders. Tom brushed against one of the rocks. He stopped and ran his hand over it. He guided Will's arm to have him touch it.

"It's not real," said Tom.

"Fake. Easily moved, and hiding something." Will

whispered. "Who in the hell are these people?"

They climbed further and the air became cooler. As the faint light of the sky disappeared, Tom realized they were in a cave. The stale air had the smell of slimy moss. *Another set of stairs.* The familiar feelings of dread and guilt filled him.

Blackness cloaked them, and the only sound was the soft drip of water. Tom pulled out his flashlight, covered it with his shirt and pulsed it on, then off. The stairs vanished into the unyielding darkness, and the tunnel made a sharp ninety degree turn just ahead.

"Keep the light off," said Will. "Let's crawl to the bend and peek around."

In coal-like gloom they groped upward with Tom keeping one hand on the knobby wall to steady himself. The cave gradually became brighter. Indistinct, at first, then more noticeable—a light ahead. Tom took a deep breath. The feeling of climbing the steps and the fear of what approached made him wish he'd never come here. But his curiosity drove him on.

His hand sensed the clammy rock changing direction. He touched Will, and they edged around the corner.

At the top of the musty stone stairway a sliver of light glowed from under a closed door. The boys crept to the door and eased it open. They entered a small room, once a closet, with another partially open door opposite them. Light flooded out and the sound of glasses tinkling and people murmuring came from beyond the opening. Their eyes met and Tom nodded. Will shook his head, but crawled with Tom across the tight space.

Lying flat, they peered through the second door. Inside, a gathering of men, and a few women, milled about, dressed like they were going to a fancy party. Tables brimmed with food including a huge chocolate cake. A waiter filled champagne glasses. Tom looked at Will and raised his eyebrows. Will shrugged. As they watched, the entire group suddenly jumped to their feet, and stared in one direction, smiling scared and fake smiles. The boys gawked trying to make out the reason.

Three men came into view. The one in the center wore an expensive suit with snow-white spats and shoes with a shine you could see from High Bridge. On either side of him were two of the biggest, meanest looking men Tom had ever seen. The man in the middle smiled back at the crowd. The other two had faces of granite. A member of the group came forward hand extended and said. "This is such an honor, Mr. Capone."

The boys eyes locked. They dared not even whisper. The short hairs on Tom's neck bristled. He remembered reading about Al Capone in the newspapers at the library. The gangster was thought to have committed murder, extortion, and robbery, but was never caught. He bribed and threatened any witnesses, and now he and his goons had come to Shakertown. And Tom knew why. All of his guesses had proven to be true. Part of him was elated, but that was overwhelmed by fear.

The group gave introductions. The lummox they called Toothy was introduced as Max, the chief of security. Capone demanded reports, and several men stood and gave information on the number of gallons and shipping times and places. The boys glanced at each other and nodded. The man who had greeted Capone explained the barge. He told of the sleeping quarters, its powerful engines, and that the locals would never imagine it carried something valuable. Capone joked about the stupid "yokels."

The leader then spoke to Capone. "Let's go down and take a look at the barge."

The gangster nodded. Tom's throat tightened. They would use the stairs he and Will came up.

"Run," whispered Will.

They leapt to their feet and bolted down the steps. The men heard the noise and flooded the tunnel with light.

"Stop!" a voice bellowed. "Get up here. Now."

But the boys kept running until a shot echoed through the tunnel. The bullet ricocheted from wall-to-wall and whizzed past Tom's ear.

Tom and Will had no choice.

CHAPTER
Fourteen

Crestfallen and terrified, the boys slogged up the stone steps and into the room filled with light and well dressed people. Everyone stared at them. Several guns were pointed in their direction.

"Why, they're just kids," said Capone. "How in the hell did you let kids get in here?" He glared at the leader with a look that would melt glaciers.

The man shuffled his feet and stammered, "I don't know, Mr. Capone, but I'll find out and heads will roll."

He walked to Will and Tom. "Who are you?"

They didn't answer, but Toothy did. "They're those kids that have been snooping around. Remember, I first saw them when they were using a telescope to look at the barge from the other side of the river. I chased them away that day, but they went to the Sheriff and then watched us from

High Bridge. They live in the West Lot house in Shaker-town."

The boys gaped at each other. Tom shuddered. Toothy knew about them.

"So I decided we better get rid of them—make it look like an accident, like the Deputy."

"You killed a Deputy?" asked Capone.

"Had to. He was spying on us. Bashed him in the head with a rock and threw him over the dam."

Tom's knees weakened as he remembered finding the body. They had suspected Toothy did it, but he was more dangerous then they imagined. Tom couldn't have been more stupid, playing games with these vicious people.

"I tried to run those kids off the road," Toothy continued, "but they got away. Then one of our men saw them get a boat and come down the river at night. I threw a big boulder in the boat. It sank and they went over the dam. The little one is supposed to be dead. He hasn't been seen for a week."

Capone's eyes drifted to the assembled group and back to the boys. A ghost of a smile played on the hard face.

"So you're hard to kill, huh?" He turned to Max, "Make sure there're dead by tonight."

Will and Tom looked at each other in terror. Toothy

spoke again, "I'll clobber them and throw them back in the river. I guarantee they'll be dead this time."

Capone shook his head. "Use your brain. If the little one is supposed to have been dead for a while, a fresh looking body in the morning is going to look awfully suspicious."

The big man blinked his eyes and frowned.

Capone shook his head in frustration and said, "Take the older one somewhere, and see if he can't fall off a cliff. Put the other one in a box and let him rot for a couple of days, *then* toss him in the river."

Toothy's eyes locked on Tom and the goon sneered. Tom's heart thudded like it was going to jump out of his chest.

Toothy and another man grabbed them by the scruff of the neck and dragged them into a dingy basement. The gangster shoved them into a windowless room and tied them to chairs. As the men started to leave Will asked, "What are you guys doing here that would bring Al Capone to Shakertown?"

"None of your damn business."

"Hey, I'm just asking. Remember I'll be dead by morning."

The big man laughed. "Yeah, you will, but I'll make you

a deal. You tell me how you got your car back down the hill so fast, and I might tell you."

Will grinned. Tom looked at him in amazement. *He's trying to con these guys. He's wasting his time, they aren't high school girls.*

"I locked the brakes and crammed it into reverse. Worked like a charm."

"I didn't know you could do that."

"Yeah, I do it all the time. Change your plans a little and I'll show you how." Will grinned again.

Toothy smirked. "No such luck, punk. I'm going to enjoy tossing you off High Bridge." Snarling now, he continued, "I can't wait to hear you splash in the water below."

The two slammed the door and locked it behind them. A wedge of light glowed beneath the door. Tom sighed and eyed Will.

"Well, I did it this time. I'm sorry, Will. It was stupid to come here. We guessed what they were doing, but I never thought we'd find a gang anywhere near this big. And with a big-time mobster like Capone running it. My bright ideas are going to get us killed this time."

"Not to worry, little cuz. We're gonna figure a way out. Start thinking. Now."

Tom twisted, scanning their prison. Even without their

hands tied, he saw no way out of this room. His stomach turned queasy as he realized this could be his tomb.

"I know one thing," said Will. "That big jackass isn't going to throw me off High Bridge. I don't know how, but I'm going to get away from him when he takes me to the trestle. Getting you outta here won't be as easy."

All too soon, the door opened and Toothy came in with his partner. He showed his snaggletooth grin to Will.

"Come on little buddy, we're going to see if you can fly."

Will grinned back. "I always thought I could."

Toothy slapped him across the face.

"Shut your smart-ass mouth. I don't want to hear another peep out of you or it's going to be harder on you than you think."

Will's face tightened and Tom knew he was seething. The toothless Goliath may have run into his David. The second man pointed a gun at Will while Toothy untied him, lifted him out of the chair, and retied his hands behind his back. They never even looked at Tom. A cold dread flowed through his body and he felt dead already.

As Will went out the door, he glanced back and winked.

CHAPTER
Fifteen

Toothy took Will outside and pushed him to the railroad tracks. The trestle spanned the river a quarter mile from the house. Plenty of time for Will to think, and he already had an idea. In silence, the man and boy walked, once stepping from the tracks for a passing freight train. Will tightened his muscles as they reached the trestle. He had one chance, and he was going to try it.

Toothy finally spoke, "Well, here you go wise ass. Time for your flying lessons."

He laughed at his own joke and grabbed Will's arm, dragging him onto the railroad bridge. Will bent his knees. He raised up quickly twisting his arm and kicking back with his foot. He connected with Toothy's knee, and broke free. He ran, across the trestle. Toothy lumbered after him. Will was gambling that the big man would remember

Capone's orders—to make his death look like an accident. But Will's back tingled waiting for a bullet. He knew he couldn't escape with his hands tied behind his back. There was nowhere to go, but he had one hope.

Toothy cursed as the man fell onto the ties with a thud. Running on the ties wasn't easy, especially in the dark, and in the rain, but Will had an edge over Toothy. He had run on the narrow bridge before.

Will kept glancing ahead, hoping for the noise and light. He took his eyes off of the cross ties and his foot missed a board. He tumbled forward trying to twist so he didn't smash his face into the tie. His shoulder smacked the rough wood, and he struggled to get up. Toothy reached him and yanked him to his feet.

"You gonna wish you hadn't done that."

Toothy punched him hard in the stomach and he collapsed onto a rail, his head dangling over the edge. The rail vibrated. Toothy hadn't noticed and jerked him up again.

"I ain't going to do anything to you that will show, but you will be begging me to throw you off this bridge."

Will's breath stuck in his throat. He breathed out as a light blinked through the trees and a train screeched onto the trestle. The man's grip loosened as the bridge shook and light from the train's headlamp flooded them. Will kicked again breaking loose and he started running, toward the train. Toothy hesitated, and plodded away from the oncoming locomotive. Will knew that dozens of trains crossed the trestle daily, and he expected one. He remembered that ladders, evenly spaced across the bridge, ran down to a catwalk. He spotted one ten feet ahead.

Will reached the ladder and stood watching as the train sped closer. He had to get off the trestle. With only one choice, he struggled to sit down, and inched forward putting one foot then the other on the top rung. He walked his feet down as far as his legs reached. Now he had to jump. He placed one foot inside the lowest rung his feet touched, and the other foot on the outside. Will gritted his teeth and leaned until he fell. With no way to stop his descent, the rung hit him in the crotch and pain surged through his body. He locked his ankles together to keep from tipping over as the train roared past him.

In agony he put his forehead against the cool railing and groaned. It was a good thing he never wanted kids. The pain rippled over him like he'd been bathed in hot sorghum. He might have to stay on the ladder until someone rescued him. Then he thought of Tom. And Toothy. *Did the monster survive?* He had to ignore the pain and climb the ladder.

Will found a rough edge on a rung. He rubbed the ropes up and down the jagged metal. Unable to see, he scratched his hands and arms several times while rubbing, but the ropes finally broke free. He gingerly climbed the rungs to the tracks. His body wobbled in pain as he warily stepped on the cross ties trying to get off of the trestle before another train arrived. In case Toothy was still alive, he reached in his boot and pulled out the .22 pistol he had wrapped in the oil skins with his clothes. The men never thought to search him. After all he was just a kid. He limped across the trestle holding the gun behind his back and watching for Toothy, waiting to throw him into the river.

He wasn't sure if he could shoot, but he might have no choice. The trestle ended with no sign of Toothy. Maybe the train got him, or he jumped.

Rocks rattled to his left. A small ledge protruded from the cliff below the bridge, and a figure stood in the gloom. The large shadow told him Toothy had escaped the train. As he tried to sneak past, a voice boomed out, "Hold it right there, I got my gun on you."

Will dropped flat and inch-wormed off the rails as the sound of Toothy climbing broke the silence. He was out of view of the man, but he wouldn't get far. Toothy would shoot him now. Will wiggled into brush and pointed his gun down the track toward the trestle. The utter blackness of the night that he and Tom wanted now worked against him. Rocks clattered in front of him as the big man approached, and then, a rumbling behind him.

The headlights of an oncoming train lit the tracks, and he made out the outline of the huge man—about twenty feet away. Will balanced his pistol with his left hand and aimed as the train neared. The noise would cover the gunshots. He had to shoot in the chest or head to stop a man the size of Toothy with a .22 caliber bullet. Sweat oozed on his palms. He quickly wiped it on his pants and re-aimed the weapon. The train headlight behind Will illuminated the giant, standing with a pistol in one hand and his other hand shading his eyes.

Will pulled the trigger.

CHAPTER
Sixteen

The door creaked and a shaft of light shot across the room. A dark figure closed the door and crept towards Tom. *This is the end. They're going to smother me so nothing will show when they find my body.*

He remembered holding his breath under water and how his chest hurt. Only this time the pain wouldn't stop until he was dead. His heart raced as the figure reached him —and patted him on the shoulder.

"Hey, cuz," whispered Will. "Let's get the hell out of here."

Tom shook his head and grinned. He had no idea how Will got away, but he wasn't going to ask now. Will's penknife sliced through the ropes, and he helped Tom out of the chair. Tom's knees buckled after sitting so long, and Will's right hand grabbed him. In his left Will carried his pistol.

"Take your boots off, tie them together, and put them around your neck. There's goons everywhere, and we gotta be quieter than a sock-footed mouse."

Will led him to the door and cracked it open. The small man, Toothy's helper, stood with his eyes wide. Will snatched him by the shirt and yanked him into the room closing the door. The man tumbled to the floor.

"Get him, Tom."

Tom jumped knees first and the man wheezed as Tom knocked the air out of him. Will pounced, covering the man's mouth with his hand.

"Get the ropes," said Will.

Tom pulled a chair over, and they lifted the gangster into the seat. Will turned the lights on and found a piece of dirty cloth. He gagged the man as Tom tied his hands.

"He came to check on you and they'll miss him," said Will. "Let's go."

Will switched off the light and closed the door. He handed Tom the penknife for a weapon, and they sneaked into the house. Will knew the way and Tom followed, his eyes darting in every direction. Footsteps echoed in the hallway, and the two ducked into a side room. The rhythmic sound of someone breathing filled the space. Sweat rolled down the back of Tom's neck. The boys waited until the clomp of boots faded and they eased out. Will led, waving his gun back and forth. Tom checked behind them. He noticed the same smell that was on the barge. Will steered Tom through another doorway into a room with a set of stairs.

"The kitchen," he pointed, "and an outside door."

Will sat on the steps pulling on his boots. Tom did likewise. Will slipped the pistol into his boot.

They tiptoed up the stairway, and a murmur of voices surprised them. Will grabbed Tom's arm and they hustled back down the steps.

"Nobody there when I came in." Will rubbed his chin and glanced around the room. He pointed to sacks of potatoes. Tom quirked an eyebrow. Will hefted a sack to his shoulder and nodded to Tom. Tom understood—another con. He grabbed a bag and they struggled up the steps. The boys crested the stairway and strolled into the kitchen. The cooks paused in their work to stare.

"Hey," said one, "we don't need all those potatoes."

Will set his on the floor. "They told us to bring them here."

"Who told you?" The man's eyes narrowed as he stared at the boys.

"I don't know. We're new."

"You're kids. How come you're working here?"

The cook picked up his butcher knife and scowled at them.

Tom's throat tightened.

"We're orphans," said Will. "Runners for a protection racket. Nobody pays attention to kids. The mob hired us because we could go places older guys couldn't."

"Where'd you come from?"

"Chicago," said Will, "came in today."

"With the big guy?" The man's eyes were wide now.

"Yeah. We'll take these back down, if you don't need them."

"No, just leave them. You don't sound like you're from Chicago."

"Uh, uh," said Will. "Born here, moved to Chicago."

The man nodded at Tom. "You?"

"Cincinnati," lied Tom.

"If you don't care," said Will. "We're going to sneak out for a smoke."

"Got an extra?"

"Nah, only brought two."

A suspicious look returned to the man's face.

"I'll give you mine. They're bad for me anyway." Will's hand went to his boot. Tom tensed.

The cook shook his head, "Shit, I don't want one you keep in your shoe."

He waved them toward the outside door.

Tom closed the door behind them and started to speak. Will shushed him. He grabbed Tom by the shirt and pulled him into bushes next to the house. They both ducked low in the weeds. Will still didn't say a word. Footsteps crunched in the leaves. Two men tromped past them. *Guards*, Tom thought. After the men passed, Will whispered, "Come on."

Will jumped up and led Tom towards the rear of the mansion. He dogtrotted by the house and into a wooded area between the palisade cliffs and the railroad track. In the distance gunshots sounded and yells echoed.

"They found out," said Will.

"What happened?"

"Later."

They ran in the darkness, with branches slapping their faces and spider webs grabbing at them. Tom noticed Will ran with a limp. He started to mention it when his foot caught and he sprawled into the weeds. His arm smacked something hard, and he reached out and touched it. A metal rail. His hands groped another opposite it. The two were separated by ties—a railroad track. Will came back and stood beside Tom. "You okay?"

"Yeah," Tom whispered. "Look at this."

Will bent over and touched the tracks. He let out a soft whistle. "A rail siding coming through the woods to the house. For unloading."

"What we thought?"

"Yeah, whiskey."

"Whiskey? You mean moonshine?"

"No, not like Brent's rot gut—it's different. They're bringing in good whiskey. A couple of years ago at Uncle Fred's he brought out a bottle of whiskey and all the men had a drink. They offered me one, but Mama wouldn't allow it. I didn't recognize the smell in the barge because we figured they were making booze here, but that ain't it. They're smuggling the stuff in. And did you smell the house? The smell's everywhere. I bet they're bottling it there, too."

"Why here? In Mercer County, Kentucky?"

"Think about it. We have the main north-south rail line and the river with all its locks and dams. That barge could go all the way to the Ohio and then to the Mississippi. They could run liquor to New Orleans."

"They couldn't do that in one night."

"Maybe this barge meets another one downstream."

"Then this is like a distribution center," said Tom. "I guess it's coming in by rail from up north, maybe Canada, then they can send it anywhere."

"And I bet that house is filled to the gills with high-quality whiskey, and maybe other stuff too like gin and pure grain alcohol."

"No wonder Capone is here. This is a big deal. We got to tell somebody."

"Yeah, but right now we better save our own skins."

Will took off again and they ran for fifteen minutes. Then he slowed and edged toward the cliff. He weaved back and forth along the cliff face—searching. Their eyes were accustomed to the darkness, but Tom worried about stepping over the rock face. The river was a long way below them. Will stopped suddenly.

"I think it's right here."

"What?"

But Will already started picking his way down the hill side. Tom reluctantly trudged behind him. Tom didn't like heights and held his breath, glad he couldn't see the drop to the river.

Will seemed to be following a hint of a trail. Will lingered when they stood on a protruding ledge. He sat down and started taking off his boots.

Tom sensed the pitch-black water below him. "What the hell are you doing?"

"We have to get out of here, and this is the only way I know. We're going to jump in the river."

Tom swallowed hard. The river appeared as a bottomless pit. Like stepping into a giant grave. And the thought of falling brought back memories of that Sunday morning.

"Don't worry, I've jumped before," Will said. "Lotsa kids have."

"How many times?"

"Once."

"Shit."

"And I'd been drinking old man Brent's corn liquor when I did it, but it'll be okay, and besides I'd rather take my chances with the river than Capone."

Tom sat on the cold rock and unlaced his boots. "What happened on the trestle?"

Will told Tom how he ran from Toothy and dropped down the ladder. Tom winced.

"Toothy didn't know I had a gun," said Will, "so I was gambling after I passed him that he still wouldn't shoot me. I knew he had to be mad as a wet hen, but I hoped he would hesitate."

"Did you shoot him?"

"Yeah."

"Is he dead?"

"No, I couldn't kill him. He was close, an easy shot. Could've put a bullet between his eyes. But I couldn't."

"What did you do?"

"He was framed in the light from the train and carrying his gun in front of him. I aimed for the gun figuring that if I missed it, I'd get him in the stomach. But I hit the gun. And then I shot twice more—at the legs. He went down, but I know he ain't dead. He's too tough."

"Why couldn't you kill him?"

"I don't know, I wanted to. He deserved it. I've shot a bunch of animals, from a distance, and up close. I never felt nothing. I just couldn't kill a human. It's different."

Tom was quiet.

A train whistle blew in the distance. Voices and the sound of dogs barking rang out across the cliffs. They were being tracked!

Will whispered. "Wait for the train. It'll cover the splash."

Tom's hand shook as he took off his boots. He noticed Will pulling off his pants and shirt too. Swimming would be easier without any clothes. The two boys rolled their clothes and boots into a ball.

"Jump holding your clothes," said Will. "They might help you float."

"Oh, sure," Tom muttered.

They stood in the cool breeze covered with goose bumps waiting as voices and dogs got closer. Then the roar of a steam engine echoed through the river valley. "Separate," said Will.

The boys spread out and Will jumped. Tom hesitated, took a deep breath, and leapt into the abyss.

CHAPTER
Seventeen

Tom fell forever. At least it felt like it. He sucked in his breath waiting for an impact he couldn't see. He heard Will's splash, then his body smacked the water so hard he thought the river had frozen solid. The shock knocked the breath out of him. He tried not to panic and hung on to his clothes. Tom relaxed and floated to the surface. He gulped air, and struggled to swim. Splashes came from beside him. *Will was okay.* He battled towards the noise.

"Swim hard," said Will, "try to get out of their line of sight. We're ducks on a pond for those guys on the cliff."

Will's breathing sounded like a panting hound dog as the boys paddled with all their strength. As they swam around a downed tree, a shadow bobbed at the water's edge. A boat. Will floated alongside the wooden dinghy. He whispered to Tom, "It's not locked up." They climbed in and Will gave a low whistle. "Look, an outboard motor."

"A what?"

"A gasoline motor. Something new. I've only seen one. Read about em in a magazine. Untie us and start rowing. I'll see if I can get it started."

Tom slipped the knot off the rope and said, "You *read* about it?"

"Yeah, yeah, I read car and engine magazines sometimes. None of that silly made-up stuff you read."

"Fiction."

"Whatever, shove off."

Tom pushed the boat from the bank. He put the oars in the oar locks and bent his back to the rowing while Will tugged on the starter rope. The motor sputtered. Twice again he yanked, but the engine refused to start.

"Doesn't it have to be primed, or choked like a car?" said Tom.

"Yeah, dammit. I forgot."

Will pulled out the choke and cranked again. The outboard roared to life as lights began to crisscross the river. Barking came from the ledge where they jumped. A beam from the cliff flashed over the boat and a hail of lead flew towards them. They ducked as the bullets whizzed. Will sped up the engine, and Tom yanked in the oars. Will steered near the bank in the overhang of trees where the men above couldn't see them. They moved up the river with the putt-putt of the motor echoing across the cliffs.

The boys hauled the boat on the sand bar upstream from old man Brent's house.

"What a piece of luck," said Will, "finding this boat with a motor and gasoline."

Tom scratched his head. "I wonder ..."

"So now what, shit-for-brains? What book have you read that will get us killed next?"

"We have to have help. We're way over our heads here. I think we should go to Lexington and talk to the police there."

"Boy, you're wet behind the ears," said Will. "The Lexington cops ain't much better than our Sheriff. Some of the older boys go there to get a woman. You know—a paid-for woman. The best place was Belle Brezing. They closed that one, but there are a lot more. The guys say you not only gotta pay the girls, but the cops, too. So if the Sheriff's on the take, then Capone's gang could buy the cops. But there's somebody else."

"Who?"

"Daddy read in the paper about a new government group, the Federal Bureau of Investigation, the FBI. They don't take bribes and one of them is in Lexington."

"One? Just one?"

"Well, hell, you got a better idea."

"Nope."

"So we gotta figure out how to get to Lexington without being seen."

"Yeah, but first we have to get out of Shakertown," said Tom.

"How?"

"Take the boat?"

"No, said Will. Not enough gasoline, and Capone's thugs'll watch the river."

"How about the interurban?"

"The trolley? We have to get to Nicholasville and once we got on it, we'd be trapped for sure."

They lay quiet, thinking.

Then Tom said. "How about the Hardy's car? You got it fixed."

"How can we get it?"

"Steal it?"

"You're crazy. We'd have Capone's people and the Sheriff after us. Helen's dad might let us borrow it. But they'll be watching the roads for us, only this time they'd just shoot us rather than trying to shove us off the road."

"Can Helen drive?" Tom asked.

"I don't think so. What are you thinking?"

"If Helen drove, we could hide in the back floorboard. They won't bother her."

"Not a bad idea, but she's a girl. She can't drive and her dad certainly wouldn't let her have the car by herself."

"I know who does drive."

Will waited.

"James. He drives the pickup on the farm."

Will shook his head. "Helen's father wouldn't let a Negro drive his new car."

"Well, don't tell him who's going to drive."

"I guess he'll let me take the car again for a good reason. Worth a try. But that means one of us has to go see Helen and fess up about your death."

"Not me," said Tom. "I'd scare her showing up like that."

"Don't worry about her. Worry about your own sorry butt. If the gangsters don't get you, she'll probably kill you."

Tom tried to laugh, but the chuckle stuck in his throat. He couldn't blame her for anything she might want to do to him.

Leaving the boat on the sandbar, the two swam to shore and climbed the bank. They slowed long enough to pull on their clothes. The boys stole through the woods into Shakertown and to the Wright house. They'd be safe in the old building, and they had supplies stowed.

Tom and Will had decided they'd both go to Helen's and bring her back to the Wright house. The three of them could then devise a plan to get the car.

They climbed the tree into the house and peered out the upstairs windows to make sure no one followed them. The street was empty. After waiting until the village slept, Will removed the chair they had placed across the inside of the side door and eased into the darkness.

The two stole to the Hardy house. Blackness enshrouded it. A dim moonlight illuminated Helen's window. Tom shivered, hoping Helen's father didn't have a gun. Tom hid while Will crept to her window. They feared Helen might scream if she saw Tom.

Tom spied from the bushes as Will tapped on Helen's screen. Her light came on and with wide eyes, she peeked out her curtains. She recognized Will and her mouth fell open.

"What are you doing here?"

"We need your help."

"We? Who?"

"I'm sorry Helen, I wish I'd told you before, but Tom's

not dead. He was in danger and had to hide. Now we're both in trouble. Big trouble."

Helen's face went ashen. She let out a long-drawn shuddering sound from between clenched teeth.

"I'm so sorry," Will said again.

Now Helen's lips tightened.

"Go away, I don't care what happens to either of you. How could you do that to everyone?"

She closed the curtains.

Will tapped again.

"Please Helen, this isn't just about us. The whole town is in danger. We have to get to Lexington and tell an FBI agent."

Helen reappeared at the window. She yanked the curtain back.

"Why didn't you do that before? Why did you have to cause so much heartache?"

Will looked at his feet. "We didn't realize how we were hurting everybody. It was fun trying to figure out what was happening on the barge. Now that we know, we're scared."

Tom started. He couldn't imagine Will admitting to a girl he was scared. Tom saw the surprise in Helen's face, too.

"Let me get my clothes on."

In a few minutes she climbed out the window and the three sneaked back to the Wright house with Helen separating herself from the boys. Tom wanted to say something, but the words didn't come.

Finally Helen whispered, "Tom Wallace, I cried for you. I've never cried for any boy. I hate you."

Will tried to put his arm around her. She shoved him away. "And you're no better."

Tom mumbled, "I don't blame you. I wish we hadn't done this, and it *was* my idea."

Back at the old Shaker residence, the boys told Helen everything. She struggled to believe that they had seen Al Capone and jumped off the palisades in the dark. She wasn't happy with what they did, but she understood their reasons.

Helen didn't want to use her father's car, but they couldn't figure out any other way to get to Lexington. Her mother was out of town so she needed to persuade her father to allow Will to drive.

"Here's what we need to do," said Tom. "Will, you'll have to let James in on what's happening, then convince your dad that you need James. Helen, can you tell your dad you have an appointment and Will's going to drive you?"

Helen nodded. "I'll tell him it's a doctor appointment.

A girl thing. He'll be too embarrassed to ask for details."

"Don't give anybody the whole story," said Tom. "The gangsters might go after them. And don't mention James."

The boys escorted Helen back to her house.

At daybreak Will went to find James. He returned an hour later.

"I told James what happened and gave him a note to take to Daddy. He acted weird."

"Weird? How?" asked Tom.

"Looked funny. Said he'd drive, but didn't ask many questions. Just kept staring at me."

"Probably shocked to hear about Capone."

"Maybe, but he acted like he'd never heard of him. Seemed more interested in the FBI agent. Wanted to know how we would find him."

"That is strange. I've always thought he knows more about the barge than he lets on. Can't imagine how."

Will nodded. "I waited until he took the note to Daddy. James said Daddy read it and agreed James could have the morning off. Daddy knows he works hard."

"What did you tell your father in the note?"

"Not much. Only something bad was happening, and I had found out about it and needed to go to Lexington in secret. Asked him to trust me. I ain't asked him anything like that before, so I think that's why he agreed. And, like everybody else, he has to know something's up."

The boys waited until Helen came. She had spoken with her father, explaining she had a doctor's appointment the following day. He agreed to let Will drive. Helen told him Will would come by early, and she wanted to leave for Lexington before daybreak.

Around midnight James joined Tom and Will in the Wright house. An hour before daylight the three stole to Helen's and hid in bushes until Helen flashed a light. James and Tom dashed to the Dodge sedan and crawled into the back seat. Helen waited a few minutes and then ran out and jumped in the front with Will. Tom realized her father would be watching her get in the car.

They left Shakertown before most of the villagers were awake. Will pulled off the main road to let James drive. Helen climbed in the back. Will joined Tom in the back on the floor. James at the wheel and Helen in the back shouldn't attract notice.

They drove to an out-of-the-way spot off the highway Will had suggested. Will evaded questions about how he found the hiding place, but Helen knew. Other girls had told her. The group waited until seven before starting again to be in Lexington when the FBI office opened.

A car sped past going toward Shakertown as they drove onto the main road. Helen grabbed the armrest.

"What's wrong?" asked Will.

"Two rough looking men in a car that passed," said Helen. "Stared hard at us."

"They's turning around," said James.

"Shit," said Will.

"Whatcha want me to do?" said James. "Out run em?"

"No," said Tom quickly. "Slow down a bit and point to something along the road. Like you're just chauffeuring Helen for a drive in the country."

"Yeah," said Will. "And don't look back."

Tom kept an eye on Helen from the car floor as she nodded and pointed like she was responding to James. She was afraid, but she didn't show it.

"They're right behind us now," said James. "I peeked in the mirror."

"Slow down some more, like you're going to let them pass," said Tom.

He felt the car brake and saw Helen tense.

"They're beside us," she whispered. "Staring."

"Stare back," said Will. "Don't let them know you're afraid. Act curious."

Tom watched Helen turn toward the car and squint.

The roar of an engine told him the car had sped up.

"They passed us," said James. "Turning around again back toward Shakertown."

Helen breathed out as the car went by going in the opposite direction.

"They were gangsters, I'm sure," she said.

"Looking for us," Will said. "I bet they were told to check out any car with kids our age in it. Kept going when they figured out it wasn't me or Tom."

Tom bit his lip. Now he was liable to get Helen and James hurt.

They started into the curves going to the river. With few cars on the road Will and Tom raised up from the floorboard. Tom's legs ached, and they had a long way to go.

"Colonel Chinn's house," said Will as he pointed to the hillside. "He's the one that does the mining. And they're racehorse people too. Their son played football at Centre when they beat Harvard."

Tom squinted at the big stone house and wondered if he'd ever have a real home.

"And just beyond his is Mr. Woodman's house, a good friend of mine. Has a cute daughter too." He grinned at Helen, who yawned.

"The banker?" asked James.

"Yeah, why?"

"I'm sorry, Mr. Will," said James. "But I don't take too kindly to your banker friend. He forced friends of my mama out of their house in the Dix Valley. Made them sell, and they didn't want to."

"That don't sound like Woodman," said Will. "He's always been fair to everybody, colored or white."

"Don't know nothing 'bout that. He ain't being fair now."

Tom was surprised at James's openness. The boy must feel comfortable with them, or he's learning from Rose.

An hour later they pulled into Lexington and drove to the address Will gave James. Sweat formed on Tom's upper lip as he wondered if this FBI person could be trusted, or would he run to the gangsters. Capone had the money to buy anybody.

CHAPTER
Eighteen

James drove to the rear of a federal building and pulled over in an empty alley. Will had found a news article in the Harrodsburg paper telling about the FBI office opening. The newspaper had listed the address. The boys jumped out their eyes darting in all directions.

"James," said Will. "You stay with the car like a chauffeur would, and Helen, you wander the streets shopping. Don't act suspicious."

Helen sighed. "We know. Get going before somebody sees you."

Tom and Will eased in a side entrance and paced down a hallway. The boys entered a closet-size space that had FBI hand-lettered on the door. Plaster cracks zigzagged down the wall and the floor needed refinishing. Thread-bare curtains covered a single window.

A young woman sat at the desk in the center of the tiny room. She faced another door to their left and gave them an uninterested look as they stood waiting.

Will approached her. "We'd like to see the FBI agent, please."

"And what is the nature of your visit?" the woman said in an official voice.

"We got a big problem over in Shakertown."

The woman picked up a pencil. "And the problem is?"

"We'd rather tell the agent," said Will.

"I'm sorry, he's busy. He doesn't have time to waste with a couple of boys."

Will glanced at Tom and sidled up to the side of the woman's desk. Tom eyed her and figured she was in her twenties. Her dress was businesslike, but her hair was the new flapper style that the city girls wore. Her dark eyes twinkled.

Will leaned over and whispered to her, "You think this ain't important, but my daddy owns a farm in Mercer County. And we're gonna lose it because of rustlers. The whole county is corrupt, and we can't trust anybody. Daddy read about the FBI and wanted to talk to the agent, but he's afraid to leave. Somebody might burn down the barn. That's why he sent us here."

He pointed to Tom. "He's my cousin. An orphan. And if we lose the farm he'll have nowhere to go."

Will smiled like the Cheshire cat.

Tom wasn't sure she was buying it, but she was charmed by Will and smiled back.

"Okay I'll tell him you need ten minutes. It'll be up to you to convince him to give you more time." Her eyes sparkled. "And I'm sure you can do it."

She pushed her chair back and ambled towards the closed door. Will tilted his head and leered. Tom was sure she noticed.

The FBI agent stomped out of the office. Will and Tom locked eyes. They were shocked that he looked so young. He was dressed in a cheap pinstriped suit, white shirt, and tie that didn't match. His coat bulged on the left side. To Tom, his eyes appeared older than the rest of him.

"I'm Rick Sweeney, FBI agent," he said. "Who are you, and why are you here?"

Will glanced at the secretary standing by the doorway.

"It's confidential," he said.

Agent Sweeney nodded and indicated for the boys to follow him into his office. He motioned with his hand toward two chairs. Tom saw the set of his jaw. He was not happy about being interrupted by teenagers.

Tom's eyes drifted to a photograph of a middle-aged couple on a bookshelf behind the agent. He hadn't seen many photos, but the quality of this picture amazed him. Sweeney followed his gaze.

"My parents," he said, his voice brittle.

Tom knew. Something had happened to them.

Agent Sweeney then glared at them and said in a curt tone, "I don't have time for games, what is this all about?"

Will jumped right in. "We have some information about the barge in the river near Shakertown."

The agent's eyebrows raised. "Go ahead."

Will and Tom explained what they had done and seen up to the night before last.

The agent nodded to Tom. "I heard you were dead. And there's something else too, isn't there?" The man's forehead wrinkled.

"Yeah, we went back last night. The cloud cover made it dark enough they couldn't spot us. We climbed on the barge and found a doorway where they unloaded something. Then followed a stairway through the cliffs to the McAllen house."

Sweeney was leaning over his desk now, his eyes wide.

"At the top of the stairs there was a party going on. Everybody all dressed up. A man came in with two big ugly bodyguards. It was Al Capone."

The agent jumped out of his chair and in Will's face.

"Are you lying to me, boy?"

Will stood. Tom figured Will wouldn't be intimidated by an FBI agent, or anybody.

"I'm telling you what happened. Believe it, or not."

The man sat back down and grabbed his black telephone. He rang the operator and asked for a long number. Someone answered.

"This is Agent Sweeney, I need Agent Young please."

A pause.

"Bob, Rick. What's the whereabouts of Capone now?"

The man on the other end of the line responded and the agent gritted his teeth. He said thanks, and hung up the phone. Sweeney leaned over the desk again.

"Capone left Chicago by private train. They don't know where he is. I can't believe you saw Capone and lived to tell about it."

Will told him the rest of the story as the agent shook his head in amazement.

"You two are resourceful, and insane. Do you know what's going to happen now?"

"That's why we're here," said Tom, "so you can help us figure out what to do next."

Sweeney stood up again, his face red.

"There is nothing for you to do now," he said in a loud voice. "Except get out of Shakertown—quick. You are hunted men with a price on your head. I'll set you up in a safe house in Cincinnati."

The boys glanced at each other and Tom shook his head. "We're not letting those goons scare us away. This is our home."

Will raised his eyebrows and grinned at Tom.

"He just loves Shakertown, and he wants to be a boy detective."

Tom glared at Will and continued, "I *don't* like Shakertown, but we're not running away, so tell us what we can do to help."

Agent Sweeney eased into his chair again. He put his hands on the back of his head, "I don't need your help. I need you to stay out of this."

"Who's going to help you? The Sheriff is useless," said Tom.

The man leaned across his desk and pointed his forefinger at Tom's nose.

"Don't be so quick to judge," he said with a clenched jaw, "when you don't know the situation."

Tom glanced at his shoes. "Yeah, you're right. I don't

understand what's going on."

The agent slouched back into his chair and took a deep breath.

"It looks like I'm going to have to tell you what I know. To keep you from getting yourselves killed."

CHAPTER
Nineteen

As Tom and Will left the office, Tom thought how little they learned from Sweeney. The agent confirmed the men in the McAllen house were smuggling whiskey, but he hadn't heard Capone was involved. Sweeney said his plans would change, but didn't explain how.

The boys crept to the end of the alley on the main street. Helen was peering in a store window while James loitered near the car. Tom signaled James who got Helen and drove to the rear of the building. Tom and Will hurried through the alley and scrambled into the car.

"What happened?" asked Helen.

"Not here," said Will. "Let's get out of town."

Tom and Will scrunched on the back seat floorboard and James put the car in gear. On the way, Tom and Will told what the FBI man had said.

Near the outskirts of the village, James and Will switched places to keep Helen's father from seeing James driving. Beyond Shakertown they saw black smoke curling into the sky.

"I've got a bad feeling about that," said Tom. His stomach knotted and guilt filled him. If something happened to the Wallace farm, he'd blame himself for getting involved with the gangsters. He should've just left town.

Tom and James got out of the car in the woods before Will returned it. They planned to meet up at the Wright house. The two sneaked toward the hiding place. The fire blazed in a nearby field—a tobacco barn on the Wallace property. Tom remembered that Toothy found out where they lived. The big man or his goons must have followed them back to the West Lot house. Probably when they were watching the barge from the trestle.

"I guarantee you Toothy set the fire," said Tom. "Capone's people are warning Uncle Davis."

"I reckon I told you not to get involved with that barge," said James.

"How do you know so much about it?"

"Can't say, but you and Will ought to go to Cincinnati like the agent said."

"We're not leaving. Sweeney said something is going to

happen, and you know, don't you?"

James shook his head and refused to answer.

Tom and James waited at the Wright House while Will and Helen dropped the car off and came to meet them.

"Any trouble?" asked Tom as he opened the door. Tom's mouth fell open as he noticed Helen had changed into pants.

They shook their heads. "Didn't see nary a soul," said Will.

"Nobody followed you?" said James. "They could've been watching Helen's house knowing y'all are friends."

"Nah," said Will. "Nobody near the Hardy house, and we came through the woods. We're okay."

James shrugged. Tom noticed his tight lips.

The four discussed what the agent told Tom and Will. The man's main point was that they must not get involved. The FBI had plans, and the teens needed to stay out of the way.

Tom stomped around the room. "I can't stand this. Capone and his goons were going to seal me up in a box and throw Will off the trestle. I want to get even. And we know the house and grounds, Sweeney doesn't."

"Yeah," said Will. "If they wanna bust into the house, we know how they can do it. And I'd like to be there when they put cuffs on Toothy and Capone."

James shook his head. "They know what they're doing. Stay out of it."

"Tom," said Helen. "The gangsters almost killed you. You two have been lucky to escape. Please listen to Agent Sweeney and James."

Tom's shoulders relaxed. He hated to sit and wait, but Helen was right. No use taking more chances.

"Okay," he said and glanced at Will. Will nodded.

"I'm going to stay here until this blows over. Why don't the rest of you go on home?"

Helen smiled and gave him a quick hug. Tom blushed.

James eased the side door open, peeking through a slit. He staggered back as two men burst in with pistols pointing. An older man with a scar on his left cheek motioned for them to sit on the dusty couch. The other, short and stocky, stood beside him. Both were grinning.

"Well, lookee here," said the older one, "not only have we got the two troublemakers, but we got a bonus too. We knew watching the redhead would lead us to you two."

"You were the ones that stared at us on the road to Lexington," said Helen.

"Yeah, Max will be happy to see we got you."

"She stays here," said Tom. "We'll go with you, but not her."

"Sorry, little boy, but you ain't making the rules. Max put a hundred dollars on each of your heads, dead or alive. He don't care, and dead is a lot easier for us. You three are dead. But the girl, he'll want her warm."

The man screwed a silencer into his revolver. Helen's eyes were as big as silver dollars. She trembled and slid her hand down her pants to her knee. Tom's lips quivered as he went to her.

"Get away from her," the older man said. "I wouldn't want a bullet to hit her by mistake."

"Tell your boyfriend goodbye, honey," said the other. "You won't be seeing him again—alive."

Out of the corner of his eye, Tom glimpsed Will's hand edging toward his boot.

The door flew open and a voice said, "I don't think so."

They all stared. Old man Brent stood in the doorway with a Tommy gun pointed at the two men.

"Over here," he motioned to the four young people.

"Who in the hell are you?" said the tall gangster.

"Horatio Brent, United States Treasury Department."

Tom was stunned. Brent looked the same, and smelled the same, but he sounded different. Sober.

"You three go somewhere and hide. Not your homes. I'll tell your folks. And don't poke your nose out until after tomorrow. James, you're with me."

He glared at Tom and Will. "Don't do anything stupid, you've done enough dumb stuff already."

Brent and James left with the two gangsters in handcuffs.

Tom's fists were clenched as he sneaked with Will and Helen into the woods and towards the cliffs. To talk.

"All right, spit it out," said Will. "You got something rolling around in that crazy head of yours. I can tell by the look on your face. What book is it from?"

Tom kicked a rock.

"Two books. *Robin Hood* and *The Last of the Mohicans*. I'm going to attack the McAllen house tonight."

Both Helen and Will gasped, unable to speak. They stared at Tom.

"You're what?" asked Helen. "Didn't you hear Mr. Brent? We're supposed to stay inside and not do anything."

"Yeah, and if you're serious, little cuz, you've outdone yourself this time. Even I couldn't imagine you'd come up with an idea like that. And just how are you going to do this?"

"Do you know who Robin Hood is?"

"No, is he a friend of yours from town?"

Tom and Helen snickered.

"You need to get to the library," said Tom. "Robin Hood is a hero of a book based in medieval England where the Sheriff and others are corrupt. So Robin Hood and his men rob the rich and give it to the poor. They also were amazing archers."

"Now you're talking. We're going to rob somebody rich and keep it, right?" Will grinned.

"Robbing's not my plan, killing is. You heard those guys. Max wants us dead and Helen ..." He didn't finish. "I want to get them, and I don't trust anybody. Not Brent, he's a Prohibition Agent and they're all corrupt. And we don't know anything about Sweeney or the FBI. Why should we believe him?"

"Tom," said Helen. "You're right. Daddy says some of the Treasury people get paid off, but there are good ones too. Mr. Brent saved us. Why wouldn't you trust him?"

"Because he's crazier than a deranged raccoon," spoke up Will. "And how in the hell are you going to attack that house? You got a cannon?"

"Something just as good."

"What?"

"You don't need to know."

"Oh no, I'm not going anywhere until I know what you've got planned."

"I don't remember inviting you."

Will turned to Helen and rolled his eyes. "Nope, you're not doing this. If I have to, I'll get Daddy or the Sheriff and have you hog tied until this mess is over."

"Then I'm leaving now. You want to try to stop me?"

"Your sister died. That ain't no reason to kill yourself."

Tom's face turned red. He glared at Will. For a minute no one spoke.

"I caused it," Tom said.

"It was an accident."

"You don't know shit about it. Nobody does." Tom was yelling now. He gritted his teeth. "I'm going."

"Then I am too."

"No."

The two boys scowled at each other, their fists clenched. Helen stepped between them.

"Please, Tom," she said. "Don't do this. You won't have a chance. Let the agents handle it. Besides I don't think you can kill anybody. You don't have it in you."

"I did, dammit." His pupils watered as he thought of the narrow stairway and the staring eyes.

"You didn't mean to. This is different," said Helen.

"No, I'm tired of being pushed around, shot at, threatened, and almost suffocated. I've got nothing to lose. Everyone thinks I'm already dead, and I plan to kill some of the gangsters. I don't want you to go, Will. You've got your family to think of."

Will's nose nearly touched Tom's. "Listen, dumb shit. You're my family, too. And look at Helen, you idiot. She cares about you. If you're stupid enough to do this, I'm going with you."

Tom shook his head.

"You've got no choice. I'll stick to you like sorghum on toast."

Tom tightened his fists again. Then his shoulders slumped.

"Will, I don't want anything to happen to you. I've already done too many stupid things that put you in danger."

"It's always been my choice to go with you, mule butt. What do we do?"

"We'll leave the house early in the morning and cross the trestle."

"The trestle? Oh no, I'm not walking on that again. I still hurt from the last time." He glanced, embarrassed, at Helen.

"I got a better way. We'll hop the train."

Will guffawed. "You ain't got any money to take the

train, and besides they won't let us off at the McAllen house. It ain't a station."

"I didn't say a passenger train," Tom said.

Will shook his head and moaned.

"Lordy, help us. We're going to hop a train like a hobo. Where do you get these ideas? I know, I know. Books."

"You two can't fight all the gangsters alone," said Helen.

"Ha," said Will. "If they throw us in a cage full of lions, they better worry about the lions."

Helen laughed in spite of herself.

"Then I'm going, too," she said.

The boys' eyes met.

"Too dangerous," said Tom.

"I can do anything you can do and I've got a good reason to go after them too—Toothy." She visibly trembled.

Tom remembered the look in Toothy's eye when he ogled Helen on the river bank. Tom shook his head.

"It's because I'm a girl, isn't it?"

"No ...," started Tom.

Will interrupted and leered at Helen. "Yeah, as a matter of fact, you are a girl. He might not have noticed, but I did."

Helen's eyes flashed. "Shut up, Will. I'm going, or I'll go

tell Daddy what you're going to do."

"Blackmail? I don't care if you go or not," said Will. "But you know book-boy here has a habit of trying to kill us on a regular basis. I'm not going to be responsible for you."

Helen's hands went to her hips. "I can take care of myself, you jerk. Where are we going to spend the night?"

Will whistled. "We?"

"Yeah, I can't go home. And stop that infernal whistling."

"The hay barn," said Tom. "We'll sleep in the stalls and Helen can sleep in the loft.

"Okay," said Helen, and she tramped up the hill.

"Wow," Will whispered as the boys hotfooted it to catch up with her. "Daddy's right, we should've never let them get the vote."

On the way, Tom crept to a storage shed where he kept a few of his things he brought from his grandfather's house. He came back carrying an elongated pack with a strap over his shoulder. The other two questioned him about it, but he said he'd tell them when they got to the McAllen house. He was afraid if they knew what he planned, they would try to talk him out of going again. At the barn the three made beds in the hay using horse blankets.

Tom had a hard time drifting off to sleep. He kept

thinking of the danger he was putting his friends in. And of Helen, sleeping just above him. He had never seen her wearing pants. The thought of watching her stomping up the hill toward the barn kept him awake. He wondered if Will felt the same way. He dozed and woke until his watch said two. He shook Will and whispered to Helen.

A sliver of moon peeked through the damp fog as the three crossed the fields to the tracks where the train slowed before starting onto High Bridge. While they walked, Will explained how to jump on the train. He said they couldn't just grab a handhold as a train zoomed by, or they might get their arm yanked out of its socket. They needed to sprint with the moving car and leap on. He had hopped a freight once before with older boys.

They scouted the area looking for the easiest place to run alongside the track. A whistle sounded in the distance. The train was leaving Burgin. Tom's heart pounded. Another one of his ideas that could get everybody killed. He wished he could've gone by himself. But when it came right down to it, he needed Will's resourcefulness and Helen's common sense. The blast of the steam engine's whistle shook him as the train neared them.

Will turned around and with a forced grin gave them a thumbs up. Tom sucked in a breath. Back into the lion's den, for the last time, one way or the other.

They stepped back as the engine, billowing steam, whizzed past them. The train slowed as the locomotive neared the bridge. Tom braced himself. Will charged, his legs churning, and Helen followed. Tom hesitated, bent his knees, and ran. His eyes locked on a handhold. *Grab it,* he thought, *and swing on the steps between the cars.* His foot hit a rock. He staggered. Falling meant he'd miss the train. He lurched in a crouched position trying to maintain his balance. When he regained his stride, the car had passed. He gritted his teeth and drove his feet over rocks and through grass until the fingers of his right hand clutched the bar. Dangling, he yanked with all his strength and his left hand seized the handhold. He swung up on the boxcar.

Sweat dripped from Tom's hands as the train chugged onto the trestle. He wrapped his arm around the metal bar as he stared wide-eyed at the water. From the steel steps he couldn't make out the bridge below him. He floated over the abyss and a rush of terror and exhilaration shot through him. As he held his breath in fear, the moon peeked out from the low hanging clouds. Near the Brent house figures milled around the river and boats bobbed nearby. Then a flash of light gleamed opposite the barge. The flash was similar to the light Tom saw when he and Will first approached the barge. The train rumbled off the bridge, and he tensed. The McAllen house whizzed by and the train slowed making the turn toward Wilmore.

"Now," shouted Will.

They jumped. Tom hit the ground, stumbled, and fell into briars. He checked his pack. No damage. He found the other two and saw Will limping.

"You okay, Will?" Tom asked.

"Mostly. Hurt my, ah...knee again, but it's fine."

"You, Helen?" asked Tom.

"I'm good. I've jumped out of trees higher than that. Of course they weren't moving."

"Is your bag of goodies okay?" asked Will.

"Yep," said Tom. "Let's put it to use."

CHAPTER
Twenty

Tom led them up the hill opposite the old house, staying in the trees and thickets to keep out of sight. He hesitated as the train slowed to a stop a short distance past the gangsters' hideout.

"Huh?" said Will. "Why did it stop?"

Lights flickered through the woods beside the house, and the clop of horses' hoofs echoed. Men with lanterns emerged from the foliage followed by a team of horses pulling a fancy rail car.

"Capone," whispered Tom. "He's leaving."

"And the railroad is helping," said Helen.

"They probably don't know who's in the car. Just know somebody paid for a hookup," said Will. "I bet they've been loading and unloading cars here for months."

"What do you mean, a hookup?" asked Tom.

"The railroad will take private cars on their trains for a price. The rich shits do it. Oil barons and their kind. They call or telegraph and the train stops. The railroad don't care who it is."

The car clunked as it latched onto the rear car of the train.

"What can we do?" asked Helen.

"We can't do a thing," said Will. "Only hope cuz here has some magic tricks in his bag."

They picked their way through the scrub trees and brush to the top of the low rise. The hill had once been used for pasture, but now lay fallow with the underbrush providing cover. From here, they were above the house, but not high enough to see the opposite side of the trestle. Large trees along the cliff's edge blocked their view.

Tom took the pack off his back and opened a compartment. He pulled out a four foot long bow and a quiver with a dozen arrows.

Will moaned. "That's your secret plan? That's all you've got? We're better off using my pistol."

"Robin Hood was an archer, and in *The Last of the Mohicans*, the Indians fired flaming arrows at the settlers. I'm going to catch the house on fire and stop those goons from hurting anybody else."

Will shook his head.

Tom reached into the bottom of the pack and pulled out a large wad of cotton.

"Where did you get that?" asked Helen.

"I found it in the boxes of stuff I brought with me from Grandfather's. He packed my mother's dishes in it. It's spinning cotton."

"What's it for?" she asked.

Will snorted. "I know, but I wish I didn't. You're going to tie the cotton to your arrows and light it, right? I'm risking my life for this?"

"You've got it, big cuz. I'll shoot arrows on the roof to start the fire."

"The roof is tile, knot-head. It won't burn."

Tom tensed. *Had he messed up again?* "Maybe I can ignite the brush next to the house. That might spread to the building."

"This sure is well planned."

Tom ignored his cousin and strung the bow. He pulled out the arrows and fished in his pocket for matches.

"Where did you get the bow?" asked Helen.

"It was my dad's." Tom was quiet for a minute. "I don't have many things of his. Grandfather said he made this before he died. He was going to teach me to use it when I got old enough."

Helen touched his shoulder.

"I never knew him," Tom said. "But I'm good with the bow. I practiced in the field behind Grandfather's. I can put an arrow about anywhere I aim, but this will be the furthest I've tried to shoot."

An explosion echoed in the distance. The ground trembled and a light glowed in the sky near Wilmore.

"Did the train blow up?" asked Helen.

Before the boys could reply, a group of armed men charged out of the McAllen house. They carried lanterns and tools and moved towards the bridge. As they neared the trestle, they extinguished the lights.

"What are they doing?" asked Tom.

"Something to the trestle," said Will. "Why would they ...?" His voice faded.

Helen tensed. "The agents."

"What?" said Will.

"I bet they're coming across the trestle," said Helen. "To arrest the gangsters. That's why Mr. Brent told us to stay in tonight."

"Why the trestle?" asked Tom.

"Ain't hardly any roads on this side of the river. You're right, Helen."

"But the gangsters know," said Helen.

"Someone squealed," said Tom.

"The explosion," said Will. "The tracks go over a small bridge outside Wilmore. I'm guessing Capone's people blew it up so the FBI can't follow him by rail. And I bet the rest of them are planning to escape on the barge. Fill it with whiskey and make a break for the Ohio River. They'd never be caught."

The three stared in horror in the dim light as Capone's men, armed with rifles and pistols, stationed themselves on the track. Others, carrying tools, snuck through the weeds and trees to the ledge below the trestle.

"Why are they going under the bridge?" asked Tom.

"To sabotage it?" said Helen, her voice cracking.

Tom squinted, trying to make out the men below the bridge. "The FBI must be riding a train across the trestle. We've got to warn them."

"How? And do you trust them now?" said Will.

Tom shrugged. "I guess I have to trust somebody. We have a flashlight, but they couldn't make it out from here," said Tom. "We're only high enough to see this side of the trestle."

"What if they could see the light?" said Helen. "How would we tell them what's happening?"

"I know Morse code," said Tom. "We say it's a trap. And I'm sure Brent is crossing the river to the barge. I saw boats in the water close to his house when we came across the trestle. He'll be ambushed too."

Helen twisted, her eyes searching the woods. She pointed to a tall pine tree with branches near the ground.

"I can climb that tree carrying the flashlight. You tell me what to send."

"You have to get to the top to be spotted on the far side, and that's a long way up," said Will.

"I'll go," said Tom. "I know the code."

Tom hurried to the tree and grabbed the lowest limb. He got part way up and a branch gave way under his feet. He grabbed a nearby limb and dangled.

"You're too heavy for the branches," said Will. "Come back down."

"Let me try. I've climbed taller trees," said Helen.

"In the dark?"

"No, but I can do it."

"Are you sure. No telling what's in the tree," said Will.

Helen drew in a breath.

"Hornets?" asked Tom.

"No, not in a pine. More like an animal."

Helen pulled up her pants leg to show a knife strapped

161

to her calf. She eased the hilt out of the leather case.

"Holy shit," said Will.

"Wow," said Tom. "That's some knife."

The blade was ten inches long and two inches wide. The point was sharpened on both sides.

"It's a Bowie knife," Helen said. "My dad's. I snuck it out of the house when I left. I was about to pull it out when Mr. Brent came."

Will laughed. "We're all armed." He patted the pistol in his boot.

Helen replaced the knife and crept towards the tree.

"Are you sure you want to do this?" Tom asked.

"No, but I have to."

"Leave the light off until you get up," Will warned. "Don't want them to see you. Tom, you climb as high as you can behind her so you won't have to shout."

Tom explained he would use the words dit and dah to send the code. For a dit Helen should flash the light; a dah meant to hold it on for a second or so.

Helen jumped and hoisted herself up on the lowest limb. Tom followed, but climbing only on larger branches. He heard her grunting and muttering as she fought through the dense foliage. He went up as far as he dared.

A branch broke and Helen yelped and said, "Damn."

"You okay?" he said.

"Yeah, a limb broke. I fell on my butt on a lower limb. Hurts like hell."

Tom chuckled. Helen had never cussed around him.

"Can you see across the trestle?"

"Yeah. I'm high enough to see over the trees." She paused. "And there's a train. Parked in the curve with its lights out."

"Must be the agents. Waiting for something. Maybe the boats I saw. Point the flashlight at the cab, somebody will be in there."

"I know," she said icily.

"Aim the flashlight at me first to practice. Ready?"

"Yes."

"Dah,...dit dah dit...dit dah,...dit dah dah dit."

"Good enough. Do it over and over. Keep an eye on the gangsters' lanterns. I hope they're not looking this way. If they come toward us get down quick."

"What am I sending?"

"It's the word trap."

Tom repeated the code and for ten minutes, Helen flashed the light across the river. Then she said, "The train's moving backwards. Oh, I just got a signal. It was dit dah dit."

"The letter R, received. Get out of the tree, now."

Gunfire popped and the sound echoed through the river valley. Helen jumped from the last branch and said between breaths, "Something is starting onto the trestle. Strange looking machine. And I saw shooting going on from both sides of the river. And boats. Coming across the river. Shooting at the barge."

"The ones I saw from the train. I wonder where the FBI got so many men?" asked Tom.

"A local posse?" said Will.

Tom shrugged. "Don't know."

The firing intensified and shots echoed from the Shakertown side toward the gangsters.

"Look," said Helen. She pointed to a dark shadow halfway out on the trestle.

"That's the machine I saw from the tree."

Muzzle flashes sparked from behind the shadow. The gangsters took cover and returned fire.

"It's a handcar," said Will. "With some kind of a shield on the front. Must be agents."

Withering fire came from the gangsters, and sparks flew like fireworks as shot bounced off the metal armor. Then, from the river below came more shooting at the handcar. The men in it ducked as the bullets whizzed.

"They're firing from the barge, too," cried Tom. "The

agents are trapped out there."

Bullets zinged off the handcart from two directions. The G-men hunkered down and didn't return fire. The gangsters under the trestle relit their lanterns and slogged through the cliff rocks toward one of the bridge's braces. They carried boxes.

"What are they doing?" asked Tom.

There was no answer, and then Helen blurted, "They must be going to blow it up. Like they did the other bridge."

Tom felt his blood turn to ice water. She was right.

"Shoot your arrows, Tom," Helen said.

"They won't go that far."

"My pot-shooter is no good at this range either," said Will.

"We have to do something," said Helen.

Suddenly, a new barrage of fire came from the river.

"Those were Springfields—like your daddy's rifle, Tom." Will said excitedly. "I can tell by the sound. Is the Army here?"

"That *was* a lot of rifles," said Tom.

The gangsters under the trestle took cover, and the others backed off the rails seeking shelter. The agents' handcart still didn't move.

"All right, I'm convinced," said Will. "It's a stalemate, so a fire might drive those rats back to the house to save their stuff. Get going, Robert Hood."

"Robin," said Tom as he notched an arrow and loosely wrapped cotton around it.

The battle intensified. Rifle, pistol, and the rat-tat-tat of Tommy-gun fire echoed through the valley.

Tom pulled back the bow, and Will lit the cotton. The arrow flew and the cotton went out. The arrow landed in the yard of the house.

Will snorted. "That didn't work so well, little cuz. Let's try wrapping the cotton tighter and let it burn longer before you shoot."

Helen snatched an arrow. "Give me that."

She expertly entwined the cotton around the arrowhead and shaft like she was braiding hair.

The second flaming arrow sailed over the tracks and hit the brick side of the house. The shaft rattled to the ground and went out.

"What are you aiming at?" said Helen.

"The front yard. I want to catch the bushes on fire. All the windows are closed."

"Yeah," said Will. The whole place is sealed up. They don't want the smell to get out. Shoot at a window. The arrow ought to break it."

"Might work," said Tom, "if the cotton stays lit."

Tom shot two more arrows with Will and Helen directing him. The third shattered a window on the first floor, but the flame went out.

"Put another in the same window," said Will.

"I've got four arrows left," said Tom as he yanked the last ones out of the quiver.

The first hit above the window. The second below it.

"Come on Tom, you can do it," said Helen.

Tom set his jaw and squinted. He pulled the bowstring back, took a deep breath, and released. The arrow sailed through the open window. They stared, but no glow showed in the house. Tom's shoulders sagged. Then, a light flared in the room and flames licked their way up the window curtains. Will smacked Tom's arm.

"Way to go, Robbie."

"Robin."

"Whatever. You did it."

He pounded Tom on the back.

Flames flickered in the first floor windows and a group of the gangsters rushed toward the house.

"Look," said Helen.

In the flickering gloom a hulking figure advanced

toward them. Both legs had white rags wrapped around them. The growing flames reflected off a sawed off shotgun in his arms and a pistol on his belt.

"Toothy," said Tom.

"Yeah, shooting him didn't seem to slow him down much," said Will.

"He's looking for who's shooting the arrows. He knows it's us," said Tom.

They scrunched in the weeds, hiding from Toothy as flames spread to the second floor. The big man was within twenty feet of them when a crack sounded and part of the building collapsed. Toothy turned to look at the burning house.

Tom notched the last arrow into the bowstring.

"Don't," said Will.

Tom pushed Will's hand away and drew the bow. All the rage, guilt, and hatred he had for himself, and the monster standing before him, came bubbling up in his mind. He aimed the arrow at the broad back. He would not miss.

The McAllen house exploded. The arrow flew. Will pulled Tom back and pushed Helen down as debris hurtled around them. One explosion followed another as the huge supply of alcohol ignited. Broken bottles whizzed through the air and small fires littered the hillside.

Then quiet—except for the hissing and crackling of flames. They stood and saw only a smoking hulk left of the once stately mansion. Toothy lay on the ground. The arrow quivered in a tree next to the prone man.

"You missed," whispered Will.

"I couldn't kill him."

"I know," said Helen. She squeezed Tom's arm.

Tom pulled out a pocket knife and inched toward the fallen figure. Will drew his pistol, Helen pulled her knife, and the two followed Tom. The man they called Toothy lay flat on his back with open eyes staring at nothingness.

Driven into his chest was the neck of a broken whiskey bottle.

Chapter
Twenty-One

Smoke swirled like mini tornados in a ghostly dance around the smoldering McAllen house. An eerie silence filled the valley broken only by the coughs and moans of the gangsters. Helen's hand held Tom's as the three stood in quiet horror surveying the surrealistic scene.

The handcar exited the trestle and rolled to a stop. Agents leapt out, disarming the stunned and wounded mobsters. Agent Sweeney spotted them and climbed the slope. He glared at them.

"Are you responsible for this?"

Tom nodded and held up his bow.

The agent shook his head. "Unbelievable. I don't know whether to thank you or arrest you."

He suddenly turned toward the house. "Capone, was he in there?"

"No." said Tom, "He escaped in a rail car."

"Shit." Spittle flew from the agent's lips.

Sweeney yelled to another agent who came running. He grabbed the man's shirt and shouted for him to go back across the trestle and call ahead.

"I want him caught," said Sweeney, his voice hard. He spun around and scowled at the young people again.

"Our train is coming, and I want you three on it. Now."

Sweeney turned to Toothy's body. "Max Milton, a two bit crook out of Louisville. Mean as they come. The mob found him running a protection racket. He killed a man with his fists in a bar fight."

Helen shuddered. Sweeney nodded at her. "Yeah, a tough customer. Another gang caught him once and beat him up bad. That's how he lost his teeth. The Louisville police said he didn't have a gold tooth when he was in their city. Capone's people paid him well."

They plodded down the hill dodging broken bottles and scorched roof tiles. Sweeney motioned to another agent. "Make sure they get on the train."

The man nodded.

Sweeney walked a bit further with them then eyed Tom and Will. "You helped us—a lot. We'd planned to bring in more agents and go after them next week. When you told me about Capone, we decided to attack immediately and try to catch him.

You two turned out to be heroes, but you just as easily might have killed our people."

He pointed his finger at them. "Think about it. What would have happened if our men followed the gangsters into the tunnel? Blowing up the house helped our agents. We only had a few wounded, but it could have gone very wrong. You were lucky, real lucky. You not only could've gotten yourself killed, but some of us. Doing what you did without telling anyone was extremely foolish."

His eyes bored into Tom. "No matter your reasons, none of you needed to take the chances you did. There are other ways to help besides putting your lives at risk."

He paused, still looking at Tom. "Don't destroy your life because of something in the past."

Tom's eyes drifted to his feet. *He's heard what I did,* Tom thought, *but he has a past too. I wonder if he wants to talk about his.*

"Who was firing the Springfields?" asked Will.

"Former Negro soldiers. Brent talked to Mr. Jefferson. He's a vet of the Civil War you know."

Tom faced Will. "Old man Jefferson we saw Junior bullying?"

172

"Only Jefferson in town," said Will. "I didn't know he was a vet. He must be older than he looks."

"He was a kid in the war," said Sweeney. "A flag bearer. Got shot up kinda bad."

"And Negro soldiers were in the Great War?" asked Tom.

"Yeah, the Shakertown soldiers were in a Negro Battalion that held their flank when the Germans broke through in France. They took huge casualties, but because of their shooting ability the Germans didn't advance. Horatio Brent knew the story, and asked Mr. Jefferson to organize them if they were willing to join the fight. They agreed, and they still had their Army Springfields."

Will shook his head. "I never heard that either."

The agent cuffed Tom on the shoulder, smiled, and started away.

"Agent Sweeney," said Tom.

The agent stopped.

"Who was flashing the light warning the gangsters?"

The FBI man hesitated. "You really are observant."

Sweeney rubbed his chin. "You earned the right to be told. It was Leon. Said he didn't know what they were doing, they just paid him to watch the river. We won't charge him. Davis vouched for him."

The FBI agent left them to help get the captured gangsters on the train.

"That crummy son of a bitch," Will spat. "I wish Daddy would fire his ass, not protect him."

Tom didn't answer. He felt a tightness in his chest. Toothy's vacant eyes troubled him, reminding him of the other death. Around him injured men lay on the ground and debris from the house littered the hillside.

He didn't expect this to happen—he really didn't want to kill anybody. He planned to burn the mansion down, and he figured the gangsters would leave the county. He never thought about the liquor exploding. He wondered if he had killed anyone besides Toothy. He may not have killed the man with his bow, but he did cause the death. The second time in his fourteen years.

CHAPTER
Twenty-Two

The green speckled bass bait smacked the side of a rock on the bank and bounced into the water.

"Use your wrist, not your arm," said Horatio Brent.

Tom reeled in the lure and glared at Will who sat smirking in the back of the boat. Brent had suggested a late afternoon fishing trip. He had agreed to teach Tom to cast since Will had no patience with his awkwardness.

"Tell you what, little cuz," said Will. "We'll just get a few rocks from shore and you can bean any fish that dares to surface."

"You're doing okay," said Brent. "Ignore him, he's been fishing all his life. Anything takes time to learn."

"Yeah," said Will, "but at the rate he's going the only way he's gonna catch a fish is if the bass die laughing."

Brent chuckled, and Tom reeled his bait back to the boat.

Tom pointed his rod at Will. "Mr. Brent, you're sitting next to the number one bullshitter and con man in the state of Kentucky. And you better keep an eye on your pocket watch."

Brent laughed. "Well, after what you did, I'm proud to know you both—whatever you are."

Will snorted. "We've always known who *we* are, but you sure fooled everybody. How did you manage to live in that rat hole of a house and be drunk and dirty all the time?"

"Wasn't easy. Made *myself* sick sometimes. I kept the back room toward the river neat and at least slept in a clean bed. That's why I didn't let you see it, Will. But the worst part was drinking the rot gut."

"Yeah," said Will. "Every time I ran into you, you sure seemed drunk."

"I wasn't drunk, but I'd sucked down enough of that poison to act like it."

"So you spied on the barge from the back room?" asked Tom.

"Sure did. Had a telescope aimed at the barge. I was watching the night you got captured and I saw the giant shadow of Max on the trestle chasing a boy and guessed you were in trouble. Figured your only escape was jumping from the palisades. I had watched kids leaping off the ledge. I didn't think you stood a chance, but I tied up my boat and motor at the tree. Just in case."

"I *knew* it," said Tom pulling back his pole. He flicked the lure with his wrist and followed through pointing the tip of the rod at the bait. It splashed in a shallow pool at the edge of the bank. Tom twitched the rod and the bait disappeared.

"Whoa," said Will. "A big one."

Tom yanked and felt the weight of the fish. The tip of the pole bent and the line moved towards the center of the river.

"Loosen the brake a little," said Brent.

Tom twisted the knob and allowed the fish to pull out line. A way to tire the fish. Tom battled with the powerful creature for ten minutes. He finally got it alongside the boat and Brent netted the jerking fish. The largemouth bass flopped on the bottom of the boat.

"Woo-ee," said Will. "I've never caught a bass that big. I take it all back little cuz, you ain't a half bad fisherman. We'll eat good tonight."

Tom grinned and pointed at Brent. "I had a good teacher."

Tom sat down to let Will fish for a while. They passed

under High Bridge and Tom asked, "Who was in the boats? That wasn't the Negroes, was it?"

"No," said Brent. "They were a group of men from the village led by your Uncle Davis and James."

"James?" the boys said in unison.

"Yep, he swam over to the barge at night and got us information. Right before the battle, he took wire across. Wrapped it around the boat's propeller so they couldn't escape. He also made several trips across the river spotting for our men in the boats. He'd then swim alongside our boats and tell them where the gangsters were on the barge and bank."

"How did he do that?" Will interrupted. "The current's too strong."

"He's a powerful swimmer. Been swimming all his life. Says he can swim near the dam without going over."

Will whistled. "And why didn't they see him?"

Brent laughed. "James said he didn't have to smear mud on his face like you two did."

"Weren't the men in the boat nothing but sitting ducks?" asked Will.

"No. We used an old ferry boat as a shield for Davis's men. They crossed the river while the gangsters were pinned down by the Negroes. But our people couldn't get on the barge until you blew up the McAllen house and diverted the gangsters. The agents then boarded the barge and captured those mobsters. A few were in the tunnel. They staggered out stunned when the house exploded. Some got away."

"Did anyone besides Toothy die in the explosion?" Tom asked tentatively.

"Apparently not. They were all out fighting us."

Tom let out a soft breath.

"Will they be back?" asked Will.

"I don't think so," said Brent, "and I'll tell you why. The mob works in places where they can intimidate people. That didn't work here.

The whole village helped. Young and old, white, and Negro. The goons that escaped will tell the big boys in Chicago. Shakertown has a secret weapon. Its people, including you two, and Helen. You saved our bacon. Yeah, Sweeney's upset with you, but he knows many more people would have been killed without your help. Like you, the village was afraid, but when the time came, they acted. You should be proud of your town."

Will smiled at Tom as if to say, I told you so.

Tom relaxed and the sun warmed his face. He glanced toward the Dix River. Construction of the new dam had started, but from the river everything looked the same. The people of the valley would lose their homes, changing their lives forever. The same way his had been changed.

His eyes focused on a large flat area below the top of a cliff. A row of tombstones glowed in the evening light surrounded by knee-high grass and spindly trees.

Tom's pulse raced. Then the familiar coldness flowed through his veins as he spotted a narrow wooden stairway between a cleft in the rock leading to the graveyard.

"Hey cuz, what's the matter? You're as white as a sheet."

"I'm okay," mumbled Tom.

Will saw the stairs. "Don't worry about that now. You're a hero."

Tom nodded trying to calm his breathing. Several people in the village had waved at him earlier in the day as he walked toward Shaker Landing. They thought he was a hero too, because he killed a man. Would this cause them to forget the other death? And what about September, in high school?

Fallen down Shaker warehouses lined the river bank. Derelicts from another time. Built by men and women with a vision of the future. He had no vision and maybe no future. Theirs lasted only a short while, but they had something to believe in. Will had the farm and Shaker-town. Tom had nightmares and stairways.

"I still want to leave, Will." He turned to Brent. "We heard something about a reward."

"Yep," the Treasury agent said. "Fifty dollars each from the Federal Government for helping to capture alcohol smugglers."

Tom's face brightened. "That's enough to get me to Cincinnati and pay for a room until I find a job."

"But you've picked up on what's happening at Dix Dam haven't you?" asked Will.

Tom cocked an eyebrow.

"Strange shit. Machinery breaking down, stuff being stolen. Daddy thinks it may be sabotage. And the company is bringing in a bunch of Negros to work. A lot of the local folks is upset."

"So?"

"A new mystery, squirrel brain, and more excitement. Just what you like."

"Not interested, got other plans."

"Figuring out how to get outta here?"

"Yep. But I'm taking your advice first. Going on a date with Helen."

Will whistled. "Damn, I've been trying forever to get

her to go out with me. Where are you taking her?"

Tom grinned. "To the library."

End

Look for the next Shakertown Adventure, *Steps Into Darkness*.

Someone is sabotaging the building of Dix Dam. When an explosion designed to destroy equipment almost kills the boys, Tom and Will join forces with FBI agent Sweeney to unravel the mystery. Lost treasure, a racial incident, and a myriad of suspects, all trying to kill the boys, lead to non-stop excitement.

Author Comments

While this story is fiction, the locations are not.

The High Bridge trestle exists and is still in use as a major north-south train bridge. The railroad added an additional track and rebuilt the bridge in the late twenties. A walkway was added so people could walk out on the bridge. However, trespassing on the trestle is not allowed. The railroad has installed cameras and will have anyone on the bridge arrested.

The catwalk beneath the bridge as depicted in the story is fiction. It never existed.

The Shaker Village at Pleasant Hill is now a restored village welcoming tourists from all over the world with lodging and dining. Much of the farm land around the old town has been preserved and is in use as a working farm. The West Lot house is real and is open for guests although it looks much different from the way it was in 1923. It has been restored to the original Shaker design as built in the 1800s. Guests can stay on the third floor where Will and Tom fictionally lived.

Over the years the fourteen locks and dams on the Kentucky River have been alternately open and closed, and today Lock #7 near Shakertown is closed. At the time of the story, 1923, it probably would have been in operation. I chose to have it closed for the purposes of the book.

On August 18, 1920, the Nineteenth Amendment to the Constitution was ratified. The amendment stated: "The right of citizens of the United States to vote shall not be denied or abridged by the United States or by any State on account of sex.

Congress shall have power to enforce this article by appropriate legislation."

The ratification came after years of struggle by the "suffragettes" including physical abuse and harassment. After the amendment, many men, as depicted in the story, opposed women voting.

Here's a link from the National Archives to resources for teachers on the amendment: http://www.archives.gov/education/lessons/woman-suffrage/

African American soldiers did play a significant role in The Great War, World War One. The most famous was the 369th Regiment, the Harlem Hellfighters. I found a few references to Kentucky black soldiers in the war, but many more resources are available. One I used is *Scott's Official History of the American Negro in the World War* by Emmett Jay Scott. The book is out of copyright and is free on

Google. It indicated that 11,320 black soldiers from Kentucky served.

Al Capone was one of the most notorious gangsters of the twenties era. However, there is no evidence that he ever came to Kentucky. Bootlegging was prevalent in the state, and smuggling happened, but a mob based activity on the Kentucky River is pure fiction. A book with an excellent chapter on Capone and alcohol is *Only Yesterday: An Informal History of the 1920s* by Frederick Lewis Allen. It is available in paperback or ebook.

Please contact me at ben@BooksByBen.com for questions or comments about the book. I'd love to hear your thoughts, and especially if you have knowledge of the area and its history. I'm available to speak to schools and groups about the book.

Ben Woodard

Study Guide

A Stairway To Danger

By

Ben Woodard

Study Guide for A Stairway to Danger

Synopsis of the story:

In A Stairway To Danger by Ben Woodard, fourteen-year-old Tom Wallace has started living with his cousin Will on his father's farm. He struggles to fit in with farm life when the boys discover a decayed body. The corpse unnerves Tom because of what happened to him before he came to the farm. In the midst of his struggles, the boys stumble on a mystery that Tom believes only he can solve.

The mystery hinges around an old barge that appeared suddenly in the Kentucky River. No one in the small town knows why it's there, but Tom is convinced that it is involved in the death. He and Will investigate the barge and find that its secret is far bigger and much more dangerous than they ever imagined. Risking their lives several times, they find themselves face to face with people who want them dead. After attempts on their lives by a giant assailant, they enlist the help of an FBI agent who warns them to stay away from the barge. They don't, and become immersed in a frightening battle between two powerful groups. And the boys with their friend, Helen, become the keys to the outcome of the epic struggle.

*　*　*

Comprehension questions for Section 1 – Chapters 1-6

1. Why has Tom come to live with Will on his farm in Shakertown?

2. What event or problem does the author use to get the story started? Why do you think he chose this event?

3. Tom is dramatically affected by what Will and he discover. Why was Tom so unnerved by this event?

4. Tom thinks the sheriff is lying. Why would the sheriff not be honest about what he knows?

5. How does the author use italics in the story? In what ways does this enhance the reader's insight into the characters?

6. What was your first impression of Tom and Will from chapters 1 and 2?

7. Discuss the setting for the story. Be sure to include time and place. Using this time period, discuss other historical events happening in

Kentucky and around the world.

8. When Tom discusses his curiosity about the barge with James, Tom gets the impression that James knows more about it than he is letting on. What connection could there be?

Vocabulary for Section 1

1. Staggered

2. Loathing

3. Derelict

4. Ambled

5. Lecherous

6. Dilapidated

7. Slogged

8. Vantage

9. Haints

10. Bellowed

11. Gingerly

12. Sculled

Comprehension questions for Section 2 – Chapters 7-12

1. Will says Tom has a death wish. Do you agree or disagree? Explain.

2. Who is telling the story? Why do you suppose the author used this point of view for the story? How would the story change if Will was telling the story?

3. Would you describe Tom's pretending to be dead as brave or foolish? Explain.

4. What additional information have you discerned from these chapters?

5. The boys believe there is a connection between the barge and the McAllen mansion. Express your thoughts on what this connection could be.

6. Would you have gone along with Tom's

scheme to enter the barge? Explain.

7. Name three events so far in the story that you, the reader could describe as suspenseful; events that made you wonder if this time the boys had gone too far. Defend your choices.

Vocabulary for Section 2

1. Indication

2. Engulfed

3. Groped

4. Extortion

5. Lummox

6. Lumbered

7. Palisades

Comprehension questions for Section 3 – Chapters 13-18

1. Some characters have only small parts in a story

but play key roles. Name such a character and explain why his/her contribution was vital to the plot.

2. If you could give Tom some advice, what would you tell him and why? Will?

3. Think of your 2 main characters. Of the two, do you feel more of a connection with Tom or Will. Explain your choice.

4. There are many conflicts that appear timeless and universal. Discuss a conflict from the book that would fit into this category.

5. Were there any parts to the story so far that seemed improbable. Does the setting (time and place) play a role in making them more feasible. Explain.

6. Does the story create a certain mood or feeling? What is it and how does the author achieve it?

7. Predict what you think really happened and why on that fateful Sunday morning at Grandfather's. Use clues from the story.

Vocabulary for Section 3

1. Confidential

2. Intimidated

3. Slouched

4. Deranged

5. Guffawed

6. Exhilaration

7. Sabotage

Comprehension questions for Section 4 – Chapters 19-22

1. Was there any event in this last section that surprised you? Discuss the event and explain why it surprised you

2. Did the story end the way you expected? Were there clues the author provided to prepare for the ending? What were some of the clues?

3. Now that Tom has the reward money, do you think he will stay in Shakertown? Support your ideas.

4. Pretend you are a new character in the story. Discuss who you are and what role you will play

in this book. How would this change the outcome of the story?

5. Compare Tom and Will. Discuss how they are alike and how they are different.

6. Most stories reflect on aspects of human nature. In what way do the 2 main characters remind you of people you have known or experiences you have had?

7. What questions would you like answered by the author after reading this book?

Vocabulary for Section 4

1. Hunkered

2. Stalemate

3. Surrealistic

4. Unison

5. Quivered

6. Hotfooted

7. Trestle

8. Withering

Possible research topics to coordinate with a Social Studies unit:

1. 19th Amendment – women's right to vote

2. Prohibition

3. Jim Crow laws

4. Underground Railroad

5. Al Capone/bootleg whiskey

About The Author

Ben Woodard

A spellbinding storyteller of high adventure, Ben has walked the Great Wall of China, hiked in Tibet, and climbed to 18,000 feet on Mt. Everest. And recently learned to surf in Hawaii.

This book sprang from stories family members told him about growing up in Shakertown, Kentucky. Tales of lost gold and river caves, and of adventure.

He began writing for children in 2008 and has completed picture books, middle grade and young adult stories.

Ben lives in Kentucky with his wife Lynda. For more information about Ben, please visit BooksByBen.com

TURN THE PAGE FOR AN EXCERPT FROM

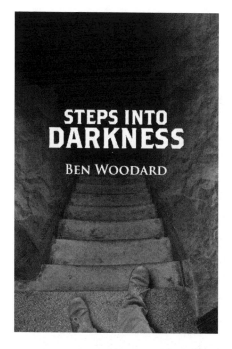

STEPS INTO DARKNESS

Book 2 of the Shakertown Adventure Series

Ben Woodard

His back was to them as he connected the wires to the detonator. Will shoved Tom. Only minutes remained.

They located the last connection point where the blasting caps were wired to two sticks of dynamite. The wires to the plunger snaked up the hill. The connecting strands were twisted, tightly, as with pliers. Tom snatched a rock, but Will grabbed his hand and pointed up the hill. Tom understood. The man would hear the pounding. They each took a twisted connection and tried to pry it apart with their fingers. They would need to break only one.

The wires resisted. Tom gritted his teeth, then remembered his pocket knife. He pulled it out, flipped the blade open, and wedged the tip between two strands. He twisted and the blade snapped. The sound startled the man. He whirled around and stared directly at the boys. Tom forced the broken blade into the gap in the wires. Will put his finger on top of one and pulled as Tom twisted. Blood ran down Will's hand as the metal bit into his finger. They strained, and watched the man. His eyes darted in all directions. Then he made his decision. He pulled the plunger up, hesitated a moment, and slammed it down.